DOC SAVAGE'S AMAZING CREW

William Harper Littlejohn, the bespectacled scientist who was the world's greatest living expert on geology and archaeology.

Colonel John Renwick, "Renny," his favorite sport was pounding his massive fists through heavy, paneled doors.

Lieutenant Colonel Andrew Blodgett Mayfair, "Monk," only a few inches over five feet tall, and yet over 260 pounds. His brutish exterior concealed the mind of a great scientist.

Major Thomas J. Roberts, "Long Tom," was the physical weakling of the crowd, but a genius at electricity.

Brigadier General Theodore Marley Brooks, slender and waspy, he was never without his ominous, black sword cane.

WITH THEIR LEADER, THEY WOULD GO
ANYWHERE, FIGHT ANYONE, DARE EVERYTHING—
SEEKING EXCITEMENT AND PERILOUS ADVENTURE!

THE MIDAS MAN

A DOC SAVAGE ADVENTURE
BY KENNETH ROBESON

BANTAM BOOKS · TORONTO · NEW YORK · LONDON

A NATIONAL GENERAL COMPANY

THE MIDAS MAN

*Bantam Book / published by arrangement with
The Condé Nast Publications Inc.*

PRINTING HISTORY

Originally published in DOC SAVAGE *Magazine August 1936
Bantam edition published March 1970*

( )

Published simultaneously in the United States and Canada

*Bantam Books are published by Bantam Books, Inc., a National
General company. Its trade-mark, consisting of the words "Bantam
Books" and the portrayal of a bantam, is registered in the United
States Patent Office and in other countries. Marca Registrada.
Bantam Books, Inc., 666 Fifth Avenue, New York, N.Y. 10019.*

PRINTED IN THE UNITED STATES OF AMERICA

CONTENTS

Chapter I

THE MAN WHO VANISHED

THE American public gets many of its ideas about what is going on, from the newspapers. Newspapers sometimes make mistakes, so the public, on occasion, fails entirely to get the true significance of things that are happening. It was thus in the Jethro Mandebran case.

Maybe it was just as well that the public did not catch on to the true significance of the Jethro Mandebran affair. A good many heads might have turned gray.

Jethro Mandebran vanished on Sunday afternoon on his private golf course. He knocked his ball into the rough, which was a patch of woods, and went in after it. That was the last they saw of him. It was utterly confounding. A swarm of private detectives could find no tracks. Some one finally thought of the old-fashioned idea of using bloodhounds, but the dogs picked up no trail.

The newspapers broke out their biggest headline type, because Jethro Mandebran, in the staid city of Philadelphia, amounted to something.

As a matter of routine, an examiner, on Monday morning, began checking the books of the bank which Mandebran owned—The Mandebran Trust Company. That afternoon, they took the examiner to a hospital, a potential nervous wreck.

There was slightly more than twenty million dollars missing.

When this came out, not a newspaper in town carried the story. They were afraid to. Such a colossal shortage in the accounts of one previously as honest as Jethro Mandebran smacked of impossibility. The editors of the journals, visioning big libel suits, would not allow a word in their columns. But after a corps of examiners corroborated the findings, the front pages of the newspapers could hardly hold the story.

An examiner who liked the bright light of publicity gave out a list containing the names of those whose money was among the missing funds. The list was a long one. It contained the name of almost every prominent person in Philadelphia, as well as numbers of financiers in New York, Boston, and elsewhere.

Clark Savage, Jr., was the three hundred and seventy-sixth name on the list.

The next day, Clark Savage, Jr.'s name as a loser made the headlines. Clark Savage, Jr., was the stuff that newspaper copy is made out of. Most of the journals, however, instead of calling him Clark Savage, Jr., designated him as Doc Savage.

The mention of Doc Savage's name in the newspapers led to his being involved in one of the most incredible adventures of a remarkable career.

NEWSPAPER reporters and cameramen made a rush for a headquarters which Doc Savage maintained on the eighty-sixth floor of New York's most distinctive skyscraper. They were met at the door by a tall bag of bones who wore a suit many times too large. A monocle with a thick glass was attached to this man's coat lapel by a ribbon. He received a certain deference from the newspaper reporters, which was surprising, reporters usually being unimpressed by big-shots.

The string of bones with the monocle was William Harper Littlejohn, one of the most famous archæologist and geologists. He was asked where Doc Savage could be found.

"Prognostication effectuates diaporesis," the bony gentleman replied.

One journalist, fortunately, carried a pocket dictionary, so the reporters managed to gather that these seventeen-dollar words were meant to convey that Doc Savage's present whereabouts was a puzzle to the bony gentleman. Further questions got more replies that had to be translated. Approximately half an hour elapsed before it dawned on the reporters that they were being kidded and told nothing.

The scribes then retired to the nearest bar, which happened to be on the corner, and swapped information.

There was conjecture about what could have happened to Jethro Mandebran. Had he vanished of his own accord? Did he have the twenty millions with him in a couple of motor trucks, which would probably be the size of the vehicles necessary to haul away such a sum? Why had a man previously so honest done such a thing?

These newspapermen later had occasion to remark on just how far wide of the facts were their conjectures on this occasion.

Not one of the journalists guessed anything near the incredible truth!

When the collective conversation shifted to such subjects as the horse races, and the pet insanities of certain city editors, two men detached themselves from the group. They did this casually. One of the pair carried a large press camera. The other wore a suit which needed pressing, and had a vest pocket stuffed full of copy pencils.

As a matter of fact, the man was not a reporter. Neither was his companion a news cameraman.

THE two mysterious gentlemen held a conference outside, covering up with the business of lighting cigarettes.

"Not so hot, huh?" muttered the one with the camera.

"You said something," agreed the other. "That skinny gink with the big words was not putting out information. I believe Doc Savage is taking a hand in the Mandebran business!"

"But how could he have gotten wise?"

"Maybe he isn't—entirely."

"You figure he don't know how big the thing really is?"

"Probably not—yet."

"Then we gotta make him stop nosin' around before he finds out too much!"

"Yeah," the man with the seedy suit and the pocket full of copy pencils agreed. "That's the chief's orders."

"You got any ideas," demanded the first, "about how to do it?"

"I always got ideas," said his companion. "Come on."

They now walked rapidly down a side street, and got in a certain taxicab which had been waiting for them. The driver of the cab was a casual-mannered young man, with a face which was noteworthy for its absence of chin.

"The Museum of Natural History," directed one of the passengers as they got seated.

"What the hell?" snorted the driver. "You guys decided to get an education or something?"

"Stick around us," he was told, "and *you'll* get an education!"

Some three quarters of an hour later, the trio stood looking at a case in the Museum of Natural History. The case held a small plaque which, the card on the case stated, had come from the tomb of the famous Tutankhamen.

It was not a busy time for the museum. The room was empty, except for two guards.

Without appearance of undue haste, two of the men sidled over to the guards, drew blackjacks from under their clothing and swung them against the heads of the two guards. Both watchmen fell without an outcry.

The other man inserted a small jimmy under the wooden lid of the case and broke the lock. He lifted the tablet out and shoved it inside his shirt under his belt. Then he tightened his belt to hold it there.

The three men walked out of the museum with their loot, attracting no attention.

TALL, bony William Harper Littlejohn came to the door of Doc Savage's skyscraper headquarters wearing a weary expression. He also looked slightly annoyed. He had been examining the almost perfect skull of a prehistoric man, which a cowboy in Wyoming had brought to light while digging post holes. The skull was likely to prove the existence of a high type of man in America much earlier than any one expected.

William Harper Littlejohn instantly recognized two of his visitors as having been with the contingent of reporters and cameramen. The third had the attire of a taxi driver.

"Salutations," William Harper Littlejohn said, not very enthusiastically.

"I got to talkin' with them other scribblers, after we left here, and found out you were an archæologist," said the man who had played reporter. "I had a friend who died a few weeks ago, and willed me his belongings. About the only thing he had was a trunk full of junk. Old jars, tablets and such things. I thought I'd bring one of the things to you, and maybe you could tell me whether the stuff was worth anything or not."

The man now drew out of his shirt the tablet from the museum.

William Harper Littlejohn gaped at the object.

"I'll be superamalgamated!" he exploded.

"It worth anything?" demanded the fake reporter.

"Antiquity indubitable!" murmured William Harper Littlejohn.

"There's a lot more of these thing," said the fake gentleman of the press.

"Is perlustration a potentiality?" murmured William Harper Littlejohn.

The visitors looked dizzy. The one playing the part of reporter grinned.

"Don't you know any little ones?" He held up a hand with thumb and forefinger separated about half an inch. "Little ones about that long? Words, I mean."

"Can I see this trunk?" asked Littlejohn, thereby proving that he did know some small words.

"You sure can," said the reporter. "It's in my rooming house. You wanta go out?"

"Subitaneously!" agreed William Harper Littlejohn.

William Harper Littlejohn was ordinarily a gentleman of caution. His long association with Doc Savage had made him so. He was one of a group of five men, each one remarkable in his way, who had associated themselves with Doc Savage, partially for the sake of the adventure involved, but also because they had an unbounded admiration for Doc Savage.

William Harper Littlejohn was a bug on archælogy, and highly enthusiastic over this tablet. He had recognized it as genuine, and had visions of turning up a find of archæological relics.

His enthusiasm evaporated in an explosion of colored lights inside his skull, a moment after he was seated in a dark-blue taxi on the street. He did not even see the black-jack blow coming.

By the time he got himself organized, handcuffs were on his ankles and wrists, and a piece of sponge filled his mouth, strapped there with adhesive tape.

The blue taxicab threaded through city traffic. A lap robe was thrown over William Harper Littlejohn, concealing his bony form on the floorboards. He struggled, but upon receiving a kick in the ribs, desisted. He could hear his captors talking.

"That was simple," declared the captor who had played cameraman.

"Brains," said the other. "Brains is what makes the world go 'round."

Chapter II

THE MUMMY CASE BUSINESS

THE blue cab went through the Holland Tunnel into New Jersey.

William Harper Littlejohn squirmed, and managed to get hold of the floor carpet. He took a firm grip. Then he groaned loudly. The groan was to cover the sound of the carpet tearing as he ripped a piece out. He had to groan three times and strain with all of his might before he was successful. When victory crowned his efforts, he held a piece of carpet about the size of the palm of his hand.

Thanking his lucky stars for the presence of the enveloping lap robe, William Harper Littlejohn worked with the bit of carpet.

What he was doing took almost fifteen minutes.

The lank geologist's apparent inactivity had allayed the caution of his captors only a little. When he reared up suddenly, violently, they fell upon him. William Harper Littlejohn, however, struggled with great ferocity.

He managed to stand up straight and shove his head hard against the top. It broke through.

In the excitement, the men failed to note the bit of rug being flung from his manacled hands through an open window.

William Harper Littlejohn was wrestled down and received a booting for the trouble he had caused.

"We're gonna lose patience with you!" one of the men gritted.

The last half hour of the journey was through sparsely settled country. The car rolled into what seemed to be an estate. William Harper Littlejohn was now blindfolded, lifted out and carried across a porch that creaked into a house. His blindfold was removed and the sponge taken out of his mouth.

He was in a dark cave of a room. The walls were painted black, which was unusual. There was a solid black rug on the floor, which was even more unique.

But the one article of furniture was most startling of all. It was approximately eight feet long and three wide—an irregularly shaped box with a lid. William Harper Littlejohn was startled into using small words, something he rarely did.

"A mummy case!" he gasped.

A man went out, evidently to the car, and came back carrying a pair of pliers. He showed these to the prisoner.

"See these?" he demanded. "They're gonna reduce your vocabulary."

William Harper Littlejohn could hardly help seeing them; they were almost jammed in his eyes.

"An anagrammatical conjugation of exigency!" he muttered.

"There!" growled the man with the pliers. "That's what I mean! No more of them words! Them jawbreakers! For every big word you use, we're gonna pull one of your teeth. A tooth for each word we can't understand! Savvy?"

William Harper Littlejohn blinked and looked as indignant as a securely bound man could.

"I don't understand what this is all about," he snapped. "Why did you seize me?"

"You have no idea?" demanded the other.

"No!" retorted William Harper Littlejohn. "I'm completely puzzled!"

"Swell!" grinned the other. "You're gonna be more puzzled, before we get done!"

They laid hands upon the skeletonlike form of Littlejohn, lifted him, and calmly plunked him down in the mummy case.

WILLIAM HARPER LITTLEJOHN had been able to give the mummy case merely the slightest of inspection, but he had recognized it as being a genuine article. And the idea of lying in a mummy case failed to appeal to him.

"I object to this treatment!" he yelled.

"We know how you feel!" said one of the men, with grim sympathy.

William Harper Littlejohn growled, "Inacquiescence is—"

The man with the pliers sprang forward. He endeavored forcibly to pry the prisoner's mouth open. There was brisk action for several moments, during which the pliers failed to get a firm hold on any of the captive's teeth.

"I'll let that one go!" the man with pinchers decided, grudgingly. "But for every big word from now on, you lose a tooth! Listen! They call you 'Johnny,' don't they?"

"Yes," William Harper Littlejohn admitted. "But what—"

"Johnny, you just shut up and lay there!"

One of the men left the black room. It was fully half an hour before the fellow reappeared. During this interval, "Johnny" made several attempts to leave the mummy case, but was knocked back into the sarcophagus. All he could do was to lie there and glare indignantly.

The returning man bore a newspaper.

"I see Jethro Mandebran had a son who was in Europe," he declared.

"So what?" asked one of his fellows.

"So the son is tearing home to try to help find his old man," announced the fellow with the paper. "It says here that he chartered a plane and flew out five hundred miles in the Atlantic to catch a transatlantic steamer. It says his plane landed on the ocean and was hauled aboard the ship. It also says that the son is gonna leave the ship in his plane as soon as he's within five hundred miles of New York. In fact, the son is probably in the air again right now."

"I'll see if the chief has any orders about this," one of the three captors said, and left the room.

JOHNNY strained against the handcuffs, but they were too strong. He indignantly tried to push the sides out of the mummy case, but had no luck. He tried to get out of the case, but they hit him on the head with a revolver barrel.

He lay back, pain making his eyes water. He was caring less and less for the inside of the mummy case. Possibly it was only imagination, but he thought he could smell traces of its original occupant.

Johnny yelled, "Was there any trunk full of archæological relics?"

"No!" grinned the man who had practiced that deception.

"Shut up, you fool!" snapped the other. "You should have told him there was!"

"He won't dream what it's all about," retorted the first. "And, say, pal, don't be so free about who you call a fool."

Johnny addressed the fellow who had objected to being insulted. "You haven't much pride, letting him call you a fool and get away with it. Shows you're short on nerve."

The man grinned widely.

"You ain't kidding anybody, you bag of bones," he chuckled. "You're trying to start a fight. Not a chance! This guy and me are great pals, even if he does have a face built for nibbling cheese."

The other man, whose features did have something of a mousey look, shoved out his jaw, made fists with his hands, and it seemed for a moment as if there was going to be a fight after all.

The man who had gone out of the room—to get orders from the mysterious "chief," he had said—came back. He looked very cheerful.

He said, "Doc Savage really don't know a thing about this business. We made a mistake when we grabbed this bag of bones."

Johnny swallowed several times. This was the truth. *But how had they learned it?*

The man looked at Johnny. "We can't turn you loose, because you would tell Doc Savage what has happened and he would meddle. So we gotta figure what to do."

There was a silence. It did not look to Johnny as if they were doing much thinking. It looked as if they already knew what they would do with him, and it would not be pleasant.

A man demanded, "Is the Happy Skeleton business going through okay?"

"The Happy Skeleton business? Sure! No slips there."

"You fools had better quit talkin' so much," the third man told the rest.

They fell silent.

All of this conversation made not the slightest sense to Johnny.

"What do you fellows want with me?" the gaunt geologist demanded, angrily.

"Nothing now," said one of the men. "We're through with you, brother!"

"You haven't done anything with me!" Johnny looked bewildered. "I mean—nothing that made sense."

"It makes plenty of sense, if you only knew!" the other assured him.

"Then turn me loose!" Johnny ordered.

The other seemed to consider this at length.

"As soon as Jethro Mandebran's son lands in his airplane," the man said, "I think we shall shoot you."

Chapter III

THE MANDEBRAN SCION

ALEXANDER CROMWELL MANDEBRAN was, as was natural under the circumstances, a public figure for the time being, a celebrity. Alex Mandebran had been interviewed aboard the transatlantic liner and had named the airport at which he expected to land in the United States. As a result, reporters and cameramen were on hand to greet Mandebran's plane.

The airport selected was one on the outskirts of the city of Philadelphia, the metropolis from which the missing Jethro Mandebran had disappeared.

The plane was a small English amphibian, sturdily built. An English pilot employed by Alex Mandebran was at the controls, and, fairly early in the morning, he made an excellent landing. He taxied up to the hangar of the airport, and immediately the ship was surrounded by a crowd.

Alex Mandebran proved to be a large man, with an especially good pair of shoulders. He had full lips, a square jaw, and his general appearance indicated considerable physical strength. His hair was smeared with gray at the temples, despite the fact that his age had been reported in the newspapers at twenty-eight.

"Really, now, I cawn't be expected to waste much time, can I?" he said, when asked to answer questions. "Nawsty thing, you know. Fair takes my breath. I'm in rawther a hurry to get to Philadelphia and investigate the beastly mess."

Despite the affected English accent, Alex Mandebran seemed a nice enough young man.

"What do you think has happened to your father?" he was asked.

"Really, I cawn't say yet," he replied.

"What do you think has happened to the twenty million dollars?" was the next question.

"Really, I'd rawther not say as to that either," the young man murmured.

"Do you know anything at all about the case?"

"I am sure that the name of my father will be cleared in the end, oh, definitely! I am going to Philadelphia at once. I trust I shall have more to say, after I am there a short time."

A reporter inquired, "How long have you been abroad?"

"Most of my life, to tell the truth," said young Mandebran.

AT this point, a very large Negro, wearing a neat blue uniform, stepped up to Alex Mandebran and saluted deftly.

"Ah got an official cah waitin' foh yo', suh," he said.

Alex Mandebran blinked. "I do not understand."

"Police, boss," said the Negro. "They done want to be nice to yo' all. In this heah cah, yo' can make a quick trip, an' it won' cos' a cent."

Taking off his hat, Alex Mandebran ran his fingers through his hair. "The police want to question me?"

"Ah reckons dey do," said the big black man. "Ah wouldn't know."

The car proved to be a large, dark limousine. The big Negro in the uniform handed young Mandebran into the rear and got behind the wheel. The car rolled away from the airport and headed for Philadelphia.

Three other cars followed. These machines held newspaper reporters, who had orders to keep tab on young Mandebran.

The three cars of the newspapermen started out with full expectations of keeping the machine ahead in sight. They received a surprise. The dark limousine traveled faster and faster. The newspapermen pushed their cars to the utmost, but they were rapidly left behind. Within twenty minutes, the newshawks had lost all trace of the black car. Thus they missed a bit of drama which would surely have been good for headlines.

Alex Mandebran in the black car became alarmed at the excessive speed.

"I say, driver!" he called. "We are hardly going to a fire!"

This got no results. Alex Mandebran rapped sharply on the

glass which separated the driver's compartment. The big Negro piloting the machine did not even look around. The young man tried to crank the glass down. It would not budge. He endeavored to open the doors. They would not open. He tackled the windows. No luck there, either.

"What the hell does this mean?" Mandebran shrieked, completely shedding his English accent.

Getting no answer, he wrenched off a shoe and employed it to beat against the glass. The glass was like armor plate. Alex Mandebran sank back on the cushions, somewhat pale.

The black limousine had left the main highway by now, and was jouncing over rough roads. Turning off sharply into a grove of trees, it stopped. The driver got out, calmly opened the rear door.

"Damn you, whoever you are!" Alex Mandebran gritted, and leaped to the attack.

The thirty seconds or so which ensued were brisk and discomfiting to Mandebran. Not only did he fail to bear the other down with his charge, but he was seized, lifted and slammed to the earth so hard that the breath left his lungs. The captor held his wrists easily, searched him for a weapon, but found none.

"Blast you! What are—"

Alex Mandebran went abruptly silent, for he had gotten a look at one of his captor's wrists.

Some of the disguising color had been rubbed off the wrists in the struggle. The captor was unmistakably a white man.

"What's the meaning of this?" Alex Mandebran demanded.

THE reply of the mysterious black driver was to begin wiping more of the coloring off his features. He worked rapidly, employing a chemical remover which came in a tube, and which he had been carrying in a pocket.

Alex Mandebran began to stare in amazement. He all but rubbed his eyes in disbelief.

"Good night!" he gasped.

"So you recognize me?"

Alex Mandebran wet his lips. "I—I recognize you from your pictures!" he admitted, jerkily.

Alex Mandebran was now urged into the limousine, and the erstwhile Negro chauffeur got behind the wheel. The car was shortly swallowed by the woods.

Chapter IV

THE STRANGE SON

IT was around noon when a tall and very huskily built young gentleman presented himself at the office of the Philadelphia police chief and requested the privilege of an interview with whoever was in charge of the Jethro Mandebran investigation.

"What name shall I say?" inquired the reception clerk.

"Alexander Cromwell Mandebran," said the young man.

A few minutes later, the young man was confronting the police chief, district attorney, a Federal investigator, police officials and a number of newspaper reporters.

"We had expected you earlier," he was told.

"I took the wrong road," the young man explained.

The district attorney asked, "Do you object to the presence of newspapermen?"

"Not at all."

"You are Alexander Cromwell Mandebran, Jethro Mandebran's son?" he was asked.

"I think I can prove that," the young man said, and smiled slightly. "I have a number of letters." He now produced envelopes addressed to Alexander Cromwell Mandebran in assorted English and European cities. These were examined.

While the scrutiny was taking place, a newspaperman nudged his companion. Both of the journalists had been at the airport when Alex Mandebran landed, and had been with the party of scribes which had later lost the scion of missing wealth.

"Notice anything queer about friend Alex?" whispered the scribbler.

His companion examined Alex Mandebran intently. "Nope. Why?"

"Maybe it's my imagination," said the other.

The investigators handed back the letters which they had been scrutinizing.

"Satisfactory?" demanded the young man.

"Yes," he was told.

THE Federal investigator studied Alex Mandebran, then asked, "Are you married?"

"No."

"At one time you were engaged to a young woman named Sylvan Niles," the investigator stated.

Alex Mandebran looked surprised. "How did you know that?"

"We are leaving no stones unturned," the other assured him. "Sylvan Niles broke your engagement herself, did she not?"

Alex Mandebran moistened his lips, then admitted, "She did."

"The engagement was broken at a London night club, was it not?" the investigator persisted. "There was something of a scene. Sylvan Niles called you some things and threw your ring at you, did she not?"

Alex Mandebran nodded uncomfortably.

"Why did Sylvan Niles break her engagement?" the government man asked.

Alex Mandebran hesitated. He not only looked uncomfortable, but indignant.

"She caught me going out with another girl," he snapped.

Some of the reporters laughed at this, and their mirth drew a scowl from Alex Mandebran.

The district attorney now took over the questioning, asking, "You are an only child, are you not?"

"Yes," admitted Alex Mandebran.

"And, as your father's only offspring, you should be his principal heir?" the prosecutor questioned.

Alex Mandebran admitted, "I suppose so."

The district attorney took a long breath. "Then tell me," he directed, "why your father's will cuts you off without a cent."

Alex Mandebran sat perfectly still for a time. He did not look particularly disappointed.

"I did not know there was a will," he said, levelly. "Am I to understand that my father is dead?"

"Not at all," he was told. "We have no idea what's become of him."

"Then why have you opened his will?" shouted the young man.

"Because we are leaving no avenue of investigation unexplored," the other replied.

Young Alex Mandebran was now asked another question.

"Do you know the present whereabouts of your former fiancée, Sylvan Niles?" he was asked.

"I no longer have the slightest interest in Sylvan Niles," Alex Mandebran snapped.

"Did you know Sylvan Niles was here in Philadelphia?" the questioner countered.

"Good night!" exploded young Mandebran. "No!"

THE newspapermen obviously had not known Sylvan Niles was in Philadelphia either. There was a bustling among them as they demanded the young woman's address. This was given them. The young woman lived in the Salimar Apartments.

It might have been noted that Alex Mandebran listened intently to this address.

Some of the reporters now departed in a great hurry, anxious to interview Sylvan Niles.

A few more routine questions were put to Alex Mandebran. Replying to them, the young man asserted he had not the slightest idea what had happened to his father, that he considered his parent one of the most honest men living, and that he could not even hazard a guess as to what had happened to the twenty million.

"Did you know a great deal about Sylvan Niles?" he was asked.

"No, I did not," he admitted. "I realized that later. I knew practically nothing about the young lady's past."

"Did you know a man named Hando Lancaster?"

"Scarcely at all," said Alex Mandebran, quickly.

"He was Sylvan Niles employer, was he not?" prompted the interrogator.

"That was my understanding, I think,"

"Her capacity was that of laboratory assistant or secretary, was it not?" asked the other.

"Sylvan Niles told me very little about her work," replied Alex Mandebran.

"What was Hando Lancaster's business?"

"I have not the slightest idea," declared young Mandebran.

"Were you at any time jealous of Hando Lancaster?"

"Good grief, no!" gasped Alex Mandebran. "Sylvan was the one who was jealous!"

There was some further questioning, but the subjects of Hando Lancaster and Sylvan Niles were not brought up again. The questions were general ones having to do with the character of the missing Jethro Mandebran. Had he been a gambler? Had he been a chaser? Did he drink? Had he ever shown any dishonest traits? To all of these Alex Mandebran answered in the negative.

"I should like to put a question of my own," he said, suddenly.

"Of course," he was told.

"In just what form was this twenty million dollars when it disappeared?" Alex Mandebran demanded.

"In the form of unregistered bonds," the district attorney explained. "Bonds which, unfortunately, cannot be traced."

"Now, I should like to be excused," said young Mandebran.

This seemed to be agreeable, so Alex Mandebran took his departure.

PERHAPS three quarters of an hour later, a taxicab unloaded the young man two blocks from the apartment house where the police had said Sylvan Niles lived. He sauntered along the street and, under the pretense of waiting for a bus, observed Sylvan Nile's apartment house.

The apartment building was a six-story structure, neat and comparatively new-looking. Several automobiles were parked in the street in front of the structure and a number of newspaper reporters were arguing violently with the uniformed doorman. One of the scribes ducked past the doorman, and the latter pursued him. A moment later, the journalist appeared again, with the doorman maintaining a secure grasp on the seat of his pants and his coat collar.

The young man who had just arrived in the taxi glanced up and down the street and then, without undue appearance of haste, stepped among near-by bushes.

A streetsweeper was approaching, trundling his large can on wheels, and occasionally pausing to use his long-handled brush. He came opposite the bushes.

"Ps-s-st!" came out of the bushes.

The streetcleaner stopped and peered. He saw a young

man on all fours in the bushes, apparently hunting for something.

"I'm trying to find something," the young man called softly. "There's five bucks in it for you, if you'll help me."

The streetcleaner hastily trundled his can to the curbing. left it and walked into the bushes to stop and look down at the young man who was on all fours. Since the latter had not looked up, the streetcleaner had failed to see his face as yet.

"Whatcha huntin'?" asked the streetcleaner.

"It would be rather hard to explain," said the young man.

He then reached inside his clothing and brought out a small glass phial. He emptied the contents of this, a liquid, on the ground beside him. Simultaneously, he held a handkerchief over his own mouth and nostrils.

"What the heck?" demanded the streetsweeper. "You nuts or something?"

The young man made no reply to this.

The streetsweeper seemed to grow sleepy. He yawned. He shut his eyes. Then he fell to the ground and began to snore.

The young man bent over the streetsweeper and began removing the latter's rather ample white uniform. The streetcleaner was a large man, and the uniform had been made larger than was necessary for him, since he wore it over his regular clothes.

The man playing the part of Alex Mandebran donned the somewhat soiled white uniform. The cap had "Deparment of Sanitation" on the band. He pulled it well down over his eyes.

He started away, paused, then came back. From a pocket he withdrew a wallet. The contents of this must have been thousands of dollars. The man extracted a twenty, folded it, and tucked it in the sleeping streetsweeper's vest pocket.

NONE of the excited group about the apartment house paid particular attention to the large man in the white uniform of a Department of Sanitation employee who trundled his trash can past them. A great deal of microscopic trash was cleaned up in the vicinity during the next few minutes. It did not take an extraordinarily keen pair of ears to ascertain what the excitement was about.

The newspaper reporters were squabbling with the doorman. The trouble seemed to be that Sylvan Niles did not want to be interviewed. She had given the doorman ten dollars to keep the gentlemen of the press out. The reporters were trying to outbid the young woman, but the doorman had now gotten mad and was telling them specifically where they could go.

The man in the streetcleaner's uniform now trundled his trash can around to the back. He peered furtively into the delivery entrance of the apartment house. There was a service elevator, with an operator. Two newspapermen were trying to persuade the operator to take them up. They were having no luck.

The man in the streetcleaner's uniform now hurried to a neighborhood grocery store. He brought a small quantity of groceries, which were placed in a spare cardboard carton. He carried these on his shoulder, so that the box half hid his face, and entered the apartment house.

"Fourth floor," he said. "I wanta collect some money, so I gotta take 'em up myself."

This ruse got him into the apartment house. He searched rapidly and found a door with the name card:

SYLVAN NILES

He knocked on the door. There was no answer. He knocked again.

The door whipped open and a feminine voice snapped, "I told you newspaper—"

The voice stopped. The young woman stared, her eyes widening. Suddenly she drove her hand into the neck opening of her frock and brought out a small revolver. She pointed this at the man in the streetcleaner's uniform.

"Come in, Alex Mandebran," she said. "I can't think of anybody I would rather see, right now!"

Chapter V

A DIFFERENT COFFIN

SYLVAN NILES was a young woman with horror in her eyes.

She was also a young woman who achieved the unusual combination of being extremely pretty, and still managing to look efficient. She would never have made a movie actress. She was too tall. Movie directors are chary of having heroines taller than heroes.

"Come in," she repeated. Her voice was queerly hoarse.

The man in the white uniform carried the groceries in, put them on a table in the living room of an apartment which looked as if it had been rented furnished.

The girl held the revolver steady.

"I've been reading the newspapers!" she said, hoarsely. "It has come to me what this terrible thing is all about."

The young man shrugged. "If you know, you know more than I do."

"Turn around!" ordered Sylvan Niles, grimly.

"What?"

"Turn around. Put your hands over your head and press you palms against the wall. Better still, step back about four feet, and lean forward, resting your weight against the wall. I don't want you moving quickly."

The visitor hesitated, then complied. The young woman slapped a hand over his person, obviously searching for a weapon. She found none.

"All right," she said. "Now we're going places!"

"What if I don't choose to go?" the man demanded.

"I don't know," said the girl. "I might shoot you."

"They electrocute people here for that."

"They wouldn't electrocute me," Sylvan Niles said, grimly. "Not if what I suspect is true."

"What do you mean?"

"You know what I mean," she retorted. "The world thinks that Jethro Mandebran has absconded, or possibly been kidnaped. There is not the slightest suspicion of what is really behind it. If the truth should come out, right now, and the newspapers publish it—well, it wouldn't be believed."

"Why not?"

"Too incredible! Too fantastic!"

"What about Hando Lancaster?" asked the large young man.

This had a remarkable effect on the young woman. She cocked her gun.

"You *do* know what's behind this!" she gritted.

The captive shrugged resignedly.

"Raise the window!" Sylvan Niles directed.

This was done. There was a rooftop on a level with the window, but perhaps a dozen feet distant.

"You will find a long plank in the bedroom," announced the young woman. "Put it across from the window to the roof. We are leaving."

"So you had your get-away all fixed," remarked her captive.

"I have not been taking any chances," she assured him. "Get a move on!"

The plank was rather heavy, but the young man handled it with marked ease, shoving it through the window and planting the end on the roof.

"Go across," he was directed. "And do not try to run when you get on that other roof.

He obeyed. The young woman followed. The roof had been tarred and gravel sprinkled on the tar. The gravel crunched under their feet. There were several buildings in a row, all of the same height. They crossed from one rooftop to another.

"We're far enough away now so that those reporters can't see us," said Sylvan Niles. "You'll find the fire escape at the rear. Go down that."

The descent was negotiated without incident. The young woman had lowered the hammer on her revolver, but she kept the weapon convenient. When they were in the alley where they might be seen, she dropped the light coat which she had brought along over her arm so that it concealed the gun.

"This way," she said.

There was a new medium-priced roadster parked in the

street. The girl took the wheel, started the engine and pulled away from the curb.

SYLVAN NILES passed the outskirts of the city and turned into an abandoned factory of some kind. The main building was of brick. There were a few outbuildings of wooden construction, but these had practically all fallen down. A tall metal fence surrounding the place, however, was in an excellent state of repair; it was nearly a dozen feet in height and surmounted by several strands of ugly barbed wire.

The young woman got out of her car, produced a key from her purse and unlocked the huge padlock which secured the gate. She drove inside, got out and locked the gate again. Then she drove directly to a large door in the side of the brick building.

She tapped the horn button three times in quick succession. The big door opened, disclosing an utterly dark interior. The girl drove inside and shut off the engine. The door closed. An electric bulb flared on.

"Get out!" the girl told her prisoner.

The captive alighted from the machine and glanced about with interest. The building had no windows, and its walls were evidently of immense thickness. Without the light of the electric bulb over the door, it would have been very dark indeed.

The man who had opened the door and was now shutting it was worth an inspection. In fact, the poor fellow must have been accustomed to being stared at. He was a freak. His body was more nearly round than it seemed a human torso could be. He was small and his head was tremendously large. Indeed, there were times when it seemed his body and head almost corresponded in size.

He had long, pencil-thin legs. His arms and hands looked remarkably like two long weeds which had been pulled up with the roots attached. His clothing was ill-fitting.

The young woman looked at her prisoner.

"You haven't forgotten Hando Lancaster have you?" she demanded rigidly.

The prisoner bowed slightly. "Glad to see you, Lancaster."

"Like hell you are!" yelled Hando Lancaster.

His voice was as brittle as glass breaking, and he threw the words out in an utterly fierce, contemptuous manner.

"Would you be kind enough to explain what this is all about?" requested the prisoner.

"You mean to tell me you don't know?" screamed Hando Lancaster.

It became apparent that yelling and shrieking was Hando Lancaster's normal manner of speech.

"He's lying!" snapped Sylvan Niles.

"He might not be!" corrected Hando Lancaster, screaming. "We'll darn soon find out!"

The prisoner was ordered to hold his hands out. His wrists were lashed together. He was marched into an adjacent room and up a flight of stairs. At the top of the stairs, Hando Lancaster unlocked a stout door.

This door, it could be noted, was of plate steel, very thick. The room, in fact, was literally a vault.

In the center, on the floor, stood a rectangular box of some dark wood. This box looked very like a coffin.

The prisoner was forced to lie in the casketlike box.

THE man in the box now gave every evidence of being profoundly puzzled.

"What's the meaning of this?" he demanded.

"It's an old Himalayan custom!" yelled Hando Lancaster.

Hando Lancaster now left the room. He had a rather marked facility for moving silently, like a spider on a web.

It was very quiet in the vaultlike room for a few moments. Hando Lancaster, in departing, had closed the door, making the room a tomb from which, it was quite probable, there was no escape.

"Twenty million is a big haul!" the girl said, suddenly. "With it, operations could be started on a widespread scale."

"I do not know what you are talking about," said the man in the box.

The girl became very grim as she stared at him. "You're lying, of course. You must be the brains of the organization. No telling how many are working with you. Hundreds, perhaps."

"I wish you'd tell me just what you are talking about," stated the fellow in the box.

"The infernal scheme must be nipped now," the girl said, grimly. "Within thirty days, it will be too late. You'll ruin no telling how many lives!"

"You credit me with great abilities," said the prisoner.

"With this thing, you'll upset the whole course of the world!" shrilled the girl, who seemed on the point of losing control of herself. "It's hideous!"

"It is mysterious, at least," said the other.

The girl leaned forward.

"How about the Happy Skeleton?" she demanded.

"Skeleton?" The fellow in the box acted vastly surprised. "You amaze me!"

Sylvan Niles gritted, "So you claim to know nothing about the Happy Skeleton? Well, I'll tell you——"

THE heavy metal door heaved open suddenly. Hando Lancaster came flying inside. He looked more than ever like a human spider.

"Don't talk!" he howled at the girl. "Don't tell him anything!"

"Why not?" she demanded.

"Wait?" shrieked Hando Lancaster. "Watch him closely! I'll be back in a minute and show you!"

He scuttled out. His arms had a peculiar habitual movement when he walked, as if he were rolling himself along in a wheel chair.

The strange, round-bodied spider of a man came flying back almost at once. He carried a glass bottle in one hand, a wad of cotton waste in the other. The content of the bottle was alcohol, odor proved. He poured some of it on the waste, then leaned over the coffinlike box and scrubbed briskly at the prisoner's features. He also scrubbed the prisoner's hair.

Sylvan Niles leaned down and stared at the features of their prisoner.

"Good night!" she exclaimed.

Hando Lancaster glared at the girl and yelled, "It's your fault!"

"Don't squall at me!" she snapped. "Everybody makes mistakes!"

Hando Lancaster leveled an arm at the prisoner in the box.

"You're not Alex Mandebran!" he screamed. "Who are you?"

Chapter VI

THE HAPPY SKELETON

A BRITTLE tension seemed to clamp over the confines of the room.

"He's not Alex Mandebran!" gulped the girl.

Hando Lancaster looked as if he was about to attack the prisoner.

"Who are you?" he demanded.

Action was the captive's answer. He got out of the coffin-like box. The manner in which he did this was the first indication that he was an individual of amazing abilities.

His wrists were tied with thick, fuzzy cord, almost small rope. It was unquestionably stout. Yet, by levering his wrists apart, he broke the binding with ease.

Coming out of the box, he gave Hando Lancaster a violent shove. The spider-like man sailed backward, collided with the girl. They both fell, but the girl retained her gun. She made a frenzied effort to get it pointed at the late prisoner. The latter was too fast for her.

A flash part of a second later, Sylvan Niles was looking at her own empty hand with a dazed expression. She had been relieved of her weapon in a way that smacked of magic. She gaped at the tartar they had caught.

"Who—who——" She swallowed twice. "Who are you?"

"You do not know?" demanded the late prisoner. This unusual individual's voice had undergone a striking change. Previously, he had used an uncanny imitation of Alex Mandebran's voice. The tone he was using now was apparently his natural one.

The voice was not only deep and resonant, but was vibrant with an impression of controlled power.

Sylvan Niles and Hando Lancaster exchanged looks, which were not so much discomfited as bewildered. It was plain that they did not have the slightest idea as to the identity of this man.

The man picked up the girl's revolver, emptied the cartridges, then tossed the weapon to the floor.

"An examination of this coffin-shaped box should prove interesting," he suggested.

Hando Lancaster stared at Sylvan Niles. The young woman stared back.

"He doesn't know what it's all about!" Hando exploded.

"He's sure to find out!" the girl retorted. "We've got to do something."

It began to look as if they contemplated desperate measures.

"Be careful," warned their late prisoner.

He seemed on the point of saying more, but did not. Instead, he whipped to the door of the room. There was something almost inhuman about the speed with which he moved. He glanced through the door, then ducked back.

A bullet came in, richocheted from ceiling to wall to floor. Gun noise filled the building with a great whooping.

THE big man whipped back and got the girl's empty gun. He lunged to the door and threw the gun. A man squawked in a loud, shocked voice. Judging from thumps, curses and other squawks, the fellow hit by the gun fell down the stairway.

"Nobody knew I was hiding out here!" screeched Hando Lancaster.

"They are no friends of yours," said the late prisoner. "They shot the instant my form was distinguishable in the door, and before they possibly could have told my identity."

With that, he was out through the door.

Sylvan Niles looked at her companion. "You know what I think?"

"The same thing I do!" retorted Hando Lancaster.

"I have guessed who that man is!" said Sylvan Niles. She pulled in a long, shaky breath.

"We've been fooling with dynamite!" said Hando Lancaster.

"Worse than that!"

"Listen!" exclaimed Sylvan Niles.

A man was making sounds. They were wild, involuntary sounds, as if the man could not help what he was doing. Great agony seemed to have fallen upon him. The uproar ended with suggestive abruptness.

The victim had fallen forward on his face. Strangely enough, he did not seem to be exactly senseless. His eyes were open. He breathed regularly, but his arms and legs were quite rigid.

THE amazing individual who had played the part of Alex Mandebran paused a few feet from the victim he had just overpowered. He did not move for a moment. There he took from his cheeks certain wax paddings which had given the upper part of his features a beefy aspect and had made his lips seem thicker.

He straightened, and it was evident that by a semicrouch and by keeping his head drawn down, he had kept his true height from being apparent.

The thing which he did to his eyes was the most remarkable of all. From each eyeball, where it had been held by suction, he carefully removed a glass cap. These were similar to the very modern eyeball lenses which some opticians employ. But the bits of polished glass had not been there to aid vision. They were carefully colored, although not enough to hinder sight. What they accomplished was to change the color of the wearer's eyes.

Suddenly, every light went out. Intense darkness clamped down.

The interior of the big building was so quiet that few human ears could have picked up a sound. But the man who had been disguised seemed to have abilities beyond those of an ordinary mortal. He plainly detected the sound of a man shifting his position off to the right. He glided in that direction, and an instant later he struck again. His fingers were on the neck of a crouching man before the fellow became aware of any threat.

What followed would have been cause for further amazement to an observer. The mysterious one's fingers did something swift, and seemingly not very violent, to the back of the victim's neck. The unfortunate never emitted a sound. His arms and legs became rigid.

He was a victim of paralysis induced by pressure on certain sensitive nerve centers.

At that instant, a flashlight came on and the beam fell on the individual who possessed so many unusual abilities.

The sight of this person had a pronounced effect on the fellow with the flashlight.

"Lookit!" he bawled. "Old King Trouble himself!"

THERE were other men in the building, several at least. Gasps and startled curses betrayed their presence. They did not seem happy.

The man who held the flashlight dropped it. The drop did not extinguish the flash. The man ran for the door.

"Damn you!" a voice squalled at him from somewhere. "Stick with this!"

"Stick with it yourself!" barked the runner. "I'm not gettin' paid to buck *that* guy!"

Others seemed to have the same idea. "Where's the door?" yelled a man.

"Over here!" shouted the first to start running.

An instant later, the fellow got the door open, letting in light. He popped outside.

A gun started banging. One man, at least, had courage. He fired several times. The bullets clouted around the spot where had stood the one whose mere appearance frightened them so.

Then the man who had done the shooting switched on a flashlight. Daylight from the doorway did not penetrate throughout the interior of the big building.

"Douse that glim!" a man squalled. "That guy'll be able to see to shoot!"

"He never carries a gun!" barked the other.

"Well, douse the damn light anyway, so he can't see us!"

A shrill scream broke up the conversation. The giant had taken another victim on the opposite side of the room.

"I'm clearin' outta here!" one of the raiders yelled.

Came another burst of shots as some one got a glimpse of their enemy. Apparently, none of the bullets took effect. No one showed willingness to go over and make sure, however. All were working toward the door.

"Pick up the unconscious men!" ordered a fellow who seemed to be in charge. "We can't leave them here!"

Not very willingly, the others obeyed the command.

The men were scared, but they kept their heads. Had they separated and fled wildly; there would have been a good chance of their being picked off one at a time. They stuck together. When they got outside, they were in a compact group. They were carrying two unconscious men.

They kept a sharp watch on the door of the big building

as long as it was in sight. When it was shut off from view by
shrubbery, they quickened their pace. Those in the middle of
the group carried the unconscious men. Those on the outskirts kept a watch.

"We were suckers to leave the cars so far away," one complained.

"How the heck was we to know we'd run into something
like this?" another countered. "We trailed old Hando Lancaster here, but there wasn't no sign of that other—that other
guy."

"Reckon they're workin' together?" a man demanded.

"If they are, it's bad," the first said.

Suddenly, the leader of the gang emitted a bellow of anger,
waved his arms.

"What's eatin' you?" one gasped.

"We left a man behind!" the leader shrieked.

THE group stopped. In the confusion and haste, they had not
realized they were short a man.

"It's too late now," one pointed out uneasily.

"Right!" agreed the chief. "Thing for us to do is clear out
of here."

They fled. They did not follow the road, but surmounted
the high wire fence by ladders, which they no doubt had
placed there at the start of the raid. They struck out across
the fields, through brush and coarse weeds.

"The big guy is poison, from what I've heard," one muttered. "Ain't like 'im to let us get away like this."

"Maybe he's overrated," snorted another.

"A lotta birds have figured that!" retorted the first.

"Yeah?"

"There's a rumor that he don't ever kill anybody," explained the other. "But he does somethin' queer to 'em. I
know a guy that had a brother that this bronze guy got. My
pal later met his own brother on the street. The poor guy
didn't even know him. He'd had somethin' queer done to
him."

A little-used byroad appeared ahead. Two cars were
parked on it. They were big, fast machines. But neither was
new enough or expensive enough to attract undue attention.

The men piled into the cars as if they had been swimming
in an ocean and had reached lifeboats.

"Where to?" demanded one driver.

"We better check on the Happy Skeleton," said a man near the window.

"You wanta go to the Happy Skeleton now?" demanded the other.

"Yeah. Make it snappy."

The cars left hurriedly.

Chapter VII

THE DESTROYED CASKET

THE men in the cars, close as was the lookout which they had kept, had seen no one watching them. There was, however, an observer. The tall, amazingly powerful-looking man who, for a time, had been the girl's prisoner.

This individual crouched in the shrubbery near the road. His position had been quite close to the cars at their moment of departure. He was close enough, in fact, that he had been able to observe the lips of the one who had told the driver where to go.

He happened to be, among many other things, a lip reader.

The man of unusual abilities now headed back toward the large brick building. He covered ground at unexpected speed, without seeming to be in any great hurry. As he traveled, he removed more of his make-up; by vigorous rubbing, he erased most of the bleaching coat from his hands and face. Thus it was revealed that his skin had an unusual bronze color and was of smoother texture than ordinary.

His eyes, without the disguising cups of semitransparent colored glass, were like pools of flake-gold that swirled and eddied like some inner current.

Of a sudden, he began to run. His speed was amazing.

A plume of smoke had arisen from the brush ahead. It crawled straight up the sky, flattened, darkened.

The old brick building—the interior had been of wood— was burning. No doubt of that. The big man of bronze ran at great speed.

There came a sound of a car starting near the brick building.

The bronze man changed his course, veering to the right, came to a tree of fair size, caught a branch and climbed. He gained a point from which he could see the road.

The car was on the road. It had two occupants, one an individual of such gnarled physical build that he was instantly identifiable.

Hando Lancaster was fleeing in the girl's car!

Hando Lancaster's companion was a senseless man, the one Doc Savage had overpowered, and who had been left behind by his fellows.

The car sped rapidly down the road and vanished.

Doc Savage looked toward the burning building and decided gasoline was responsible for the violence of the conflagration. The girl had not fled. She had a number of five-gallon gasoline cans, and was splitting the tops of these open and throwing them at the building. She was taking chances; a moment later, she was almost burned!

That must have scared her. She gave it up, backed away and appraised her handiwork. What she saw appeared to satisfy her. The building was going to be a total loss.

THE young woman heaved a sigh, as if she were well satisfied. She threw her other gasoline cans on the roof. She played safe this time, however, for she did not open them, but threw them up intact, depending on the increasing heat to burst them.

There was little more she could do to make destruction complete. She ran through the gate, which had been left open when Hando Lancaster's car departed. Her halt was abrupt. She grabbed for her revolver, which she must have retrieved and reloaded.

But the bronze giant, who had appeared suddenly from the brush, was upon her. She tried to dodge, had no success. A metallic hand plucked the gun out of her fingers.

A brief scrap ensued. She kicked her captor's shins—kicked *at* them rather, for he dodged her kicks with uncanny ease. Looking disgusted rather than frightened, she gave it up.

Her captor remarked on the lack of fear. "You do not seem scared?"

"You have the reputation of never killing any one. Why should I be scared?"

The bronze man studied her. There was absolutely no

expression on his metallic face. "Just who do you think I am?"

The young woman shrugged. "I know you, all right!"

When his flake-gold eyes seemed to seek hers with strange power, she looked away hastily.

"And you're not going to hypnotize me!" she snapped.

"Why did Hando Lancaster leave in the car and let you remain behind?" he asked. "Why did he take that unconscious man?"

Silence was her reply.

"You had something in that building," said the bronze man. "Hando Lancaster took it away in the car. You remained behind to make sure the building burned and wiped out any traces which might have remained."

"You've added mind reading to your other accomplishments!" she said, coldly.

The bronze man must have concluded further questioning useless. He threw the gun into a ditch, then led the girl off the road. She looked scared, and struggled. He picked her up and carried her, his tremendous strength making her quite helpless.

THE reason for his leaving the road was soon apparent. A fire engine passed with a great racket. Others followed, gathered around the old brick building. There seemed to be no water available in quantity, so they employed chemical equipment.

Success was noticeably absent. If anything, the fire seemed to burn more briskly. the firemen gave it up, drew back, and devoted their attention to keeping the conflagration from spreading through the brush. This occupied them for almost two hours.

During the interval, the bronze man and his prisoner remained in the brush. He spoke only once.

"What is behind this mystery?" he asked. "What became of Jethro Mandebran and the twenty million?"

"Look in your crystal and see!" the girl suggested.

He did not ask her any more questions.

Once the blaze had burned itself out, and there were no more flying sparks, the firemen loaded their equipment and departed. A few curious persons had gathered, but these drifted off.

"Come," the bronze man said.

The girl, Sylvan Niles, obeyed because she had no other

choice. She was taken to the scene of the fire. Her captor proceeded to look around. He did a very thorough job of it.

Particularly did the bronze man devote attention to the hot ruins. He risked burning himself to scrutinize that part of the remains, where the ashes of the strange, coffinlike box would have fallen. He found nothing there. The thing had been completely destroyed.

Next, the big man circled widely, searching trash dumps in the vicinity. Prying with a long stick, he worked over their contents. Then he went back to the girl.

"Hando Lancaster has been conducting some sort of experiments here, has he not?" he asked.

"It's a pretty day, isn't it? she suggested.

THE big bronze man studied her for some moments.

"You are going to talk!"

"That's what you think!"

He grasped her right wrist and they set out down the road. His strides were long, easy, without apparent haste, but she had to trot at times to keep up.

When they came near the outskirts of the city, she brightened, apparently visioning herself calling help. But the bronze man thwarted that by tying her wrists and ankles together, despite her violent struggles. Then he gagged her. His work was effective, but not rough.

He left her concealed in a thicket.

A few minutes later, the bronze man appeared in a near-by neighborhood grocery store and asked permission to use the telephone. He made a brief call, and spoke in a voice so low that no one in the store overheard.

Then he went back to the girl. She eyed him curiously, obviously wanting to know what he had done. He did not explain.

Half an hour later, a large limousine arrived. It was the same car which had picked up young Alex Mandebran at the airport. Alex Mandebran himself was occupying the rear seat.

The car's driver was an individual who must have weighed in excess of two hundred and fifty pounds, and whose height could not have been much over five feet. He was almost as broad. Hair on his wrists was like rusty shingle nails. He had an incredibly big mouth, small eyes, and almost no forehead.

In short, the gentleman looked like an ape.

This simian apparition leaned out of the car window and

spoke in a voice that was utterly ridiculous for one of his appearance. It was a child's voice.

"Hiyah, Doc!" he said.

The girl looked intently at her giant bronze captor. "So I was right about your identity!"

The bronze man's strange flake-gold eyes studied her, but he said nothing.

"You are the famous Doc Savage," the girl repeated.

"Who's the lady, Doc?" demanded the apish man.

"Miss Sylvan Niles, this is Lieutenant Colonel Andrew Blodgett Mayfair, more frequently known as 'Monk,'" the bronze man said. "Monk is one of the world's leading industrial chemists."

The young woman looked at "Monk's" bullet of a head, and asked, "Where do you keep them?"

"What?" Monk demanded.

"The brains."

Monk grinned amiably at her, opened the door to the front seat and said, "Get in."

Sylvan Niles stared at a creature which the opening of the door had revealed. It was a pig, an entirely grotesque-looking shote with long legs, tremendous ears and a body of no consequence.

"Good night!" the girl gasped. "What's that thing?"

"That's no thing," Monk explained in an injured tone. "That's Habeas Corpus, my pet pig. Habeas, meet the lady who don't think a heck of a lot of our looks."

"She's too ritzy for me!" Habeas apparently said.

Sylvan Niles swallowed her surprise, deceived for a moment, but then realizing Monk had used ventriloquism to make it seem that the pig had spoken. She started to get in the front seat.

"She had best ride in back," Doc Savage said.

Monk's lifted eyebrows almost merged with his close-cropped hair.

The bronze man opened the rear door. Alex Mandebran, sitting inside, looked steadily at the young woman.

"You have met Alex Mandebran?" Doc Savage asked the girl.

The stare which Sylvan Niles bent on Alex Mandebran was icy. "Do I have to ride with him?"

"You do," Doc Savage told her.

With Alex Mandebran and Sylvan Niles in the rear of the limousine, Doc Savage and Monk in front, the car got in motion. It rolled into Philadelphia.

"Take the bypass road," Doc directed. "We are going on to New York."

Monk nodded. He was an excellent driver. The big machine slipped along almost noiselessly.

Doc Savage touched a button located out of sight under the dash, then put on what was ostensibly a radio headset, but which actually reproduced what was said in the rear seat. It caught and magnified even whispers, which was well, because Sylvan Niles and Alex Mandebran were whispering.

"I tell you, I came over to try to help my father!" Alex Mandebran was saying.

"Liar!"

Young Mandebran groaned. "You've got me all wrong. You seem to suspect me of something. I assure you I am *not* guilty of anything underhanded!"

"Liar!" repeated the young woman.

"I wish you'd do me the justice of telling me of what I am suspected," the young man whispered. "After all, that's only fair. You broke off our engagement in England without a reason."

"I gave a reason!"

"It didn't make sense! You said I was scheming against you and Hando Lancaster. I don't understand that. What was it all about?"

At this point, the car halted for a stop-light, and the young woman made a sudden effort to open the door and leap out.

"It's no use," young Mandebran assured her. "These doors are fastened by some kind of trick lock. I myself haven't been able to figure out how they work."

Sylvan Niles snapped, "You mean I'm a prisoner in here?"

"Call it that."

The young woman subsided with an indignant hiss.

The traffic thinned, and the car picked up speed. They got on the broad, smooth expanse of an express highway.

The loud-speaker reproduced more conversation from the rear seat.

"WHAT are you doing here?" Sylvan Niles demanded.

Alex Mandebran began, "I told you I came over to try to help locate my father."

"I mean right here in this car!"

"I am helping Doc Savage."

"Ah-h-h!" grated the girl. "Don't lie to me!"

"I'm not. Doc Savage met me at the airport. He got me away by a ruse, so that the newspapermen would not know he had met me. Later, he explained he was interested in my father's disappearance."

"Why?"

"Part of that missing twenty million is his. Some of it belongs to charitable institutions in which Doc Savage is interested."

"I see," said Sylvan Niles.

"Doc Savage wanted to investigate secretly, so the criminals wouldn't know he was on the job," explained Alex Mandebran. "He hit on the idea of going to Philadelphia, disguised as myself. I'm a large man, although not quite as large as he is. He managed a wonderful disguise. The man is a wizard!"

Sylvan Niles seemed to think the matter over.

"Sometimes I almost feel that you are honest," she admitted at last. "I know that can't be right."

Alex Mandebran protested, "Would I be working with Doc Savage, if I were a crook?"

"I don't know," said the girl. "I don't know what to think."

"Suppose you tell Doc Savage all you know," Alex Mandebran suggested.

"I'll think it over."

In time, they entered on the Skyway over the Jersey flats and approached the Holland Tunnel under the Hudson River —the entrance into New York City.

While the tolls were being paid, there were sounds of a struggle from the rear seat. Evidently the young woman was trying to attract attention by waving her arms. Doc Savage looked back. Alex Mandebran had coöperated to the extent of pulling the curtains, so that the girl's antics could not be seen. He must be holding her mouth.

They went into the noisy tunnel.

"What part of the city, Doc?" Monk asked.

"Wall Street sector," Doc Savage said. "The Miners' Building. We're going to look into the mystery of this thing they're calling the Happy Skeleton."

Monk worried the ribs of his pig, Habeas Corpus, with a toe, looked happy as he anticipated coming action.

"What we find at the Miners' Building," Doc Savage said, "should help clear up the mystery of the Happy Skeleton."

Chapter VIII

MYSTERY IN THE MINERS

THE Miners' Building was exactly what its name implied—an office structure which housed on its two-score of floors some of the world's leading mining corporations. It was a colossal structure, and the designer had striven for an effect of massive strength. There were almost no decorative embellishments.

"Drive around the block," Doc Savage directed.

"Huh?" Monk looked puzzled.

"Two carloads of men left Philadelphia headed for the Happy Skeleton," Doc Savage explained. "They were the fellows who made the attack on the brick factory building which burned."

How Doc Savage connected anything called the "Happy Skeleton" with the Miners' Building, was beyond Monk. He shook his nubbin of a head and drove as directed. Doc Savage kept a sharp lookout without it being too obvious that he was doing so.

The bronze man saw no trace of the cars used by the gang which had staged the strange attack.

"Park somewhere," Doc directed.

Monk did so.

The bronze man now alighted. The manner in which he opened the rear door of the car would have been utterly mysterious to an observer. He simply grasped the handle, turned and the door came open. It was no more complicated than that.

There was, of course, a simple explanation for the mechanism of the door's lock. Unnoticed in the palm of one hand, the bronze man carried an electromagnet. The door handle itself was of nonmagnetic brass, concealed in which was a steel plunger, well oiled. A tiny spring kept this shoved in where it engaged the lock mechanism, blocking its operation. Under the influence of the electromagnet, the bolt was drawn out against the pressure of the weak spring, leaving the lock free to operate when the door handle was turned.

It was a simple device, but one which not every individual would solve.

Sylvan Niles and Alex Mandebran started to alight. Doc Savage motioned them back, then indicated that Monk was to enter.

"Watch these two," Doc said.

"Will I!" Monk grinned, and put his pig, Habeas, in the back.

Leaving the three of them locked in the rear of the car, Doc Savage entered the Miners' Building. He consulted the directory of tenants on one wall of the lobby.

CASTELLO MINING CORPORATION

The bronze man's inspection stopped there. The Castello Mining Corporation was a big concern. Doc had an amazing memory, thanks to training by scientific methods.

Castello Mining Corporation had been in the news lately, having opened up a new vein of gold ore in their holdings in the western part of the United States. So promising had been this strike that the stock of the concern had skyrocketed. Doc Savage simply recalled having read this in the newspapers, together with the location of the concern's offices.

The gold strike had been made in the Happy Skeleton range of mountains near Death Valley, and the Castello Mining Corporation had recently been nicknamed the Happy Skeleton.

An elevator took Doc Savage to the seventeenth floor, where the offices of the Castello Mining Corporation were situated. In fact, the concern had the whole floor.

It is a common practice for visitors to business offices merely to walk in. Doc Savage did so.

A dead man lying on the floor was the first thing to meet his eye.

THE dead man was not alone. He was surrounded by a cluster of silent, staring persons, evidently company employees. There were two policemen present, and a gentleman who was undoubtedly the medical examiner. The latter was going over the body.

The corpse had a bullet hole through the head. The hole where the bullet had gone in was powder-burned. The fingers of the cadaver clutched a revolver.

"Who is he?" Doc Savage asked.

"John Maurice Castello," a policeman growled. Then he recognized Doc Savage, and his impersonal, slightly gruff attitude changed instantly. "Anything we can do for you, Mr. Savage?"

Almost every policeman in the city knew that Doc Savage held a high honorary commission on the force.

"You might answer some questions," Doc said. "Is it murder?"

"Oh, no! Not at all."

"Sure?"

"Absolutely!" said the policeman. "Castello walked out of his office, carrying a revolver in his hand. He stood right here in front of everybody and shot himself."

"There was no possible chance of foul play?"

"None." The officer suddenly looked doubtful. "None that anybody can see. You any suspicions?"

Doc Savage did not answer that. Instead, he put a question. "Any motive?"

"You bet, a darn good one!" The officer seemed on firm ground here. "A couple of months ago, this guy's mining company opened a rich vein of gold ore out West—"

"That was in the newspapers," Doc said. "The Happy Skeleton."

"The vein was a fake," explained the policeman. "It was fixed up so that the big news would boost the company's stock. They worked it very smooth, what I mean!"

"How did this come out?"

"The district attorney got a telephone tip to-day," replied the officer. "An investigator from the district attorney's office came over and talked to Castello. He threw a bluff into Castello. The man confessed that the Happy Skeleton vein was a fake!"

"The investigator was here when the suicide occurred?"

"Yeah, and is his face red! Castello said he wanted to dismiss his office employees for the day, and came out to tell them to go home. There was a policeman at the door, so Castello couldn't have escaped. He must have had a gun in his clothing. They hadn't searched him yet. He pulled it out and shot himself. That's all there is to it."

Doc Savage moved slowly about the office. He seemed in no hurry, yet his flake-gold eyes missed nothing. The late Castello's private office was marked by his name on the glass. The door was partially open. Doc Savage shoved it farther ajar and entered. He stood just inside, eyes roving.

"Has the place been searched?" he asked the policeman.

"Nope," said the officer. "We haven't got around to that yet."

"Who telephoned the tip about Castello's crookedness?" Doc queried.

"Somebody who wouldn't give a name."

The bronze man beckoned. "It might be a good idea to search this place now. Would you care to be present?"

"You bet!" said the officer, who had heard a great deal about the manner in which this bronze man worked. "We might get a line on the other one."

"What other one?" Doc countered.

"Castello had a silent partner," elaborated the policeman. "Whoever it was, he sure kept in the background. Even these employees here don't know the person's name; but we're prying around. We'll learn who it was."

"When you do, would you mind letting me have the information?" Doc Savage requested.

"Sure, we'll do that."

The bronze man had been looking over the room as he talked. It was large for an office. The furniture, as might have been expected, had been selected to create an impression of substantial richness, the background from which shysters and confidence men prefer to work.

There was an enormous mahogany desk. A straight-backed chair for visitors was situated at either end of this. Behind that was the chair apparently used by Castello. This was a great overstuffed affair of leather and wood. Probably it had cost as much as some of the minor employees of the concern earned in a year.

"We will examine that chair closely," Doc Savage said.

The results of his words were unexpected, cataclysmic. There was a flash, a terrific report. A hellish white light filled the room!

THE explosion had been rather terrific. The policeman was completely upset. Doc Savage himself had been slammed backward a few paces, but did not lose his feet.

Doc Savage lunged forward. The blast had completely demolished the chair. It seemed to be Doc's idea to get some of the fragments. He did not succeed, for a simple reason.

The room was on fire! It was an unusual kind of conflagration. It spread with incredible rapidity. The desk, which had been partly demolished, was a bundle of red flame. The carpet was burning. So were the walls.

Doc Savage changed his course suddenly, lunged, seized the policeman and dragged him out of the room to safety. He was not a fraction of a second too quick. The office was literally stuffed with fire.

The cop, while dazed, had not been knocked senseless. When Doc released him, he managed to stand.

"Whew!" he gulped. *"Whew!"*

Doc Savage seemed to have a number of things to do in a great hurry. He flashed across the office, past the excited, howling employees and policemen. In the corridor, he veered left. At the end of the elevators was a stairway. He plunged into this, descending one flight, and reached the door of the office suite beneath that of the Castello Mining Corporation. He hit the door hard. The panel caved.

This office also was a mass of flame. There was a hole in the ceiling, undoubtedly blown out by the blast upstairs.

Fire virtually covered the office. The heat was terrific. The few window panes unbroken by the blast were starting to melt and buckle. Doc Savage shielded his eyes against the white, hot glare, managed to look around enough to determine that a rather miserable desk and a pair of chairs, along with a cheap rug, had been almost the sole items of furniture. Desk and chair were already virtually burned, and the rug was filling the air with a choking stench of yellow smoke.

Doc had partially torn the door from its hinges in entering. He now finished the job, then carried the door to the end of the hall and up the stairway.

There was a great deal of excitement in the Castello offices. They were trying to fight the fire. The bronze man ignored the uproar, and took one of the police expert's fingerprint outfits, which had been abandoned for the moment, and went over the door which he had brought up. He found no finger prints.

Some one strung a water hose from the standpipe in the hallway. Water was turned through this and played on the fire. The results furnished quite a surprise. It was almost as if gasoline had been applied to the blaze.

Doc abandoned his search for finger prints, convinced there were none.

"Keep water off that fire!" he called, sharply.

They looked at him as if they thought he had gone suddenly mad.

"Then how you gonna put it out?" a cop demanded.

"It is impossible by ordinary means," Doc Savage explained. "The interior of that overstuffed chair was loaded with a type of incendiary chemical. The more water you put on it, the hotter it gets."

The officer waved his arms, bellowed, "But what—"

"The best procedure is to let it burn itself out as soon as possible," suggested the bronze man. "In the meantime, it might be a good idea to empty the building of occupants. This is a fireproof building, but the steelwork may be weakened enough to permit the roof to sag."

"We'll do that!" gulped the police officer.

HALF an hour later, the excitement had subsided somewhat. A crowd had gathered down in the street to watch smoke pouring out of the skyscraper. The assemblage had been increased by the exodus of tenants from the building.

The chemical fire had burned itself away. The interior of the office in which the explosion had occurred had been almost completely destroyed. So had the office below. The floor had fallen in, leaving only the naked girders of the building's structure. These were still red-hot, and sagged.

Doc Savage moved about in the smoking wreckage, still searching. The heat had not only melted from the windows such glass as had not been broken in the explosion, but had fused odd bits of metal. Everything even remotely inflammable had gone.

" 'Twas a death trap which some one had set for Castello," decided a police officer.

Doc made no comment.

"There was a bomb in the chair, with the chemical stuff," elaborated the policeman. "There must have been a wire or something down through the floor to the office below, where somebody was hiding and set the thing off when you were about to examine the chair. They hoped to kill you."

Doc held silence.

"Well, it was a death trap!" The officer shook his head slowly. "Crime sure don't pay! That guy Castello was fixed to get it anyway, if he hadn't committed suicide!"

At this point, another policeman approached.

"We've dug up some dope," he said.

"What about?"

"The name of the partner of this Castello."

"Who is the partner?"

"The telephone operator was lying to us before," explained the policeman. "You know how these telephone operators are. They're not supposed to talk about the firm's secrets. This one wasn't going to talk, but that explosion and fire scared her. She broke down and gave us the name."

"And are you gonna gimme that name or not?" growled the man's superior.

"Hando Lancaster."

"Eh?"

"Hando Lancaster is the partner's name."

THERE came into the room a small, weird sound. It was a note which almost defied description, not alone because it was vague, but also due to its eerie, ethereal quality. It was best described as a trilling.

Both policemen peered about curiously. It was the first time they had heard the sound, so they did not know that it belonged to Doc Savage; that it was a small unconscious thing which the bronze man did in moments of mental stress.

The trilling faded into nothingness, and, since Doc Savage offered no explanation, the source of the sound was left a mystery.

"Any further information on this Hando Lancaster?" Doc Savage asked.

"None," replied the policeman. "This telephone girl remembered the name, because one time Castello put in a long distance call to Hando Lancaster in England."

"Did she listen to the conversation?"

"She did. But what she overheard don't make any sense. Or maybe it does! I dunno. Castello wanted his partner, Hando Lancaster, to put more money into the mining company."

"What was Hando Lancaster's response."

"He refused."

Doc Savage asked a few more questions, to which he got replies that added nothing to the information which had already come to light. The bronze man now conducted another brief search of the establishment. He turned up nothing of value.

Doc entered the elevator, rode down to the street and pushed his way through the throng which was still congregated there.

Walking rapidly, Doc Savage went to the spot where he had left the limousine containing Monk, Alex Mandebran and attractive Sylvan Niles. The car was where he had last seen it. The street was wet. Evidently a sprinkler had just passed.

The machine was empty.

THE car doors were closed. Doc Savage slapped a hand swiftly into a pocket, got the tiny electromagnet which was necessary in opening the car and wrenched the door ajar. Excepting for the pig, Habeas, who grunted noises of delight when he saw Doc, the interior of the machine was indeed empty.

Indications of violence showed. The floor carpeting was wadded in a corner. The cushion lay askew. On the cushion was a wet scarlet stain. Doc scrutinized it and decided some one had been wounded.

Doc Savage withdrew from the machine.

With great suddenness, he dived inside again. Simultaneously, there was a shrill squeak, a loud clank, as a rifle bullet hit. Doc banged the car door shut just as another slug arrived.

The bronze man undoubtedly owed his life at that moment to the routine of exercises which he had taken each day since childhood. One particular part of that exercise routine had to do with development of vision and alertness of eye. Very little of what went on around him escaped the bronze man.

A man with a rifle is a distinctive figure, even when he shows only a part of himself and his weapon in a doorway half a block distant. Doc had seen him, and moved a fraction of a second before the fellow fired.

The bronze man dived forward into the front seat.

A bullet flattened against the windshield. These slabs of

glass were not much less than an inch thick, and proof against all ordinary bullets.

The key was still in the ignition switch. Doc started the motor.

Doc drove toward the rifleman. The fellow must have seen that his murder scheme had been thwarted. He sprang back in the doorway.

The district was a somewhat shabby one, despite its nearness to the financial section. The building into which the man had vanished was evidently one housing small factories and lesser wholesaling establishments.

Doc Savage wrenched swiftly in a compartment almost unnoticeable under the car seat. A drawer came out. In a tray in this. bedded in cotton, were a number of glass globes, somewhat smaller than baseballs. They held a bilious-looking liquid. Doc cranked down a window a crack, but not enough to leave himself unprotected. He tossed the glass balls through as he drove down the street.

The spheres burst on hitting the pavement, the contents splashing wetly. These damp stains evaporated, as the liquid turned into a colorless, odorless vapor. It was a gas of a type perfected by Doc Savage. It produced a harmless form of unconsciousness lasting for intervals varying from a few minutes to many hours, depending on the strength of the ingredients. The stuff was also dissipated by the air, becoming powerless in a long or short time, depending on the strength of another of its components.

Doc did not slacken the speed of the car, but drove swiftly, reached the corner and turned to circle the block. There would, of course, be a chance for the rifleman to escape into the next street. Doc was still tossing out gas grenades. It was his intention to lay a barrage of the vapor around the block.

He ran into difficulties, however. There was a traffic jam in the street at the end of the block. He saw it, stopped quickly, turned around and headed in the other direction. He escaped the effects of the gas in the street simply by holding his breath the length of the block. The gas had to be inhaled, before it would overcome any one.

Noise of racing automobile engines reached his ears. Two machines appeared in the street ahead, both open touring cars. Out of the door came the man with the rifle. He flew down the steps, across the sidewalk and hopped into one car. The automobile went into motion.

Doc Savage was half a block behind. His machine gained swiftly, for it had momentum and the other two did not. The occupants of the cars ahead began to shoot. Bullets, hitting the bulletproof windshield, made fine spidery cracks which hindered vision.

The enemy cars took the first corner, turning right, and Doc Savage got a glimpse of the occupants as they swung.

The same gang that had raided Hando Lancaster's building!

Monk, Sylvan Niles and Alex Mandebran were in the cars! Monk was a prisoner. It was impossible to be sure about the others.

Doc Savage took up pursuit. There was small likelihood of their losing him, for they had stock cars, while the special machine Doc was driving was capable of something near a hundred and fifty miles an hour.

The motor of Doc's car stopped!

Chapter IX

STOCK TRADERS

THERE was nothing indefinite about the stopping of the motor. One instant it was running, and the next it was not. Doc coasted to the end of the block, wheeled into a side street, where he would be protected from bullets, and stopped.

A bullet could hardly have cut the ignition. Radiator and hood were armor-plated, and there was dual ignition, anyway. The bronze man gave the gasoline gauge a glance. That cleared the mystery. Tank empty!

He searched, and quickly found the reason. Some one had crawled under the chassis and parted the feed line from the gasoline tank.

It was rarely that Doc Savage was taken by surprise, due to developed powers of observation, but he had been tricked on this occasion. The freshly sprinkled street accounted for it. Water from the sprinkler, of course, had floated off the gasoline, which had run from the tank; otherwise, Doc would have detected the odor.

The interval required to locate another car—it chanced to be a taxicab—was sufficient for the enemy in their speeding machines to escape. The bronze man cruised in the hack for several blocks, found no trace of those he sought, and returned.

He spoke briefly to the police, and an immediate alarm was broadcast to radio patrol cars, directing that the two tourings be picked up.

Enlisting the assistance of a squad of police, Doc Savage now went through the buildings in the block around which he had distributed the gas. Since more than fifteen minutes had elapsed, the stuff had dissipated itself. An examination of the premises showed that no one had come to harm.

Doc Savage neglected to explain to the police just what had put every one to sleep. The police knew nothing of the existence of his unusual gas. To tell them what had happened would have caused needless complications. Even Doc Savage's influence would not have preserved him from questioning and, perhaps, criticism. He avoided possible difficulties by keeping still.

The police received a telephone report from a precinct station that the two touring cars had been found, abandoned. There was no trace of the occupants.

Doc Savage went to the spot. The two automobiles stood in a little-used water-front street, literally an alley. The occupants must have changed to other conveyances, but there had been no observers.

Doc Savage went over the two cars for finger prints. There were none. Nor were there other clues.

"This is gettin' plumb mysterious," said a policeman.

The bronze man said nothing, maintaining his usual lack of emotional display.

Doc hailed a cab and went back to the spot where his own car had stalled. He picked up Habeas Corpus, who had been rooting around the back seat, and transferred him to the cab. Then Doc instructed the cab driver to go to his skyscraper headquarters.

Doc walked close enough to the big building to observe a

number of men lounging about the lobby. The fact that some of these had cameras, marked them as newspaper employees. The bronze man backtracked, with the pig following, reached the other side of the building and entered what seemed to be an innocent freight entrance into which trucks could be backed. It was really the exit from his private basement garage, and he walked down the runway, traversed a passage and took his private elevator to his eighty-sixth floor quarters.

A voice greeted him excitedly, the instant he entered.

"Doc!" the voice exploded. "There's the devil to pay!"

The speaker was a wiry man with an unusually thin waist. He had a high forehead and the large mobile mouth of an orator, but his clothing was the item about his appearance which struck the eye. The man was a sartorial miracle, his garb an array to delight the eye of any tailor.

"What is it, Ham?" Doc Savage asked.

The sartorially correct man was Brigadier General Theodore Marley Brooks, better known as "Ham"—a nickname he did not particularly care for. He was by way of being one of the nation's most astute lawyers, when he chose to practice. But he was happier adventuring with Doc Savage.

Besides Johnny, Monk and Ham, Doc Savage had two other aides, who, because their professions called them for the time being, were not in the thick of the present mystery. One was "Renny"—Colonel John Renwick, world-famed engineer; the other was "Long Tom"—Major Thomas J. Roberts, a wizard with electricity.

"It's Johnny," Ham said, in reply to Doc's question.

"What about him?"

"Let me show you."

Ham led the way from the reception room into a library, the walls of which were lined with bookcases, holding ponderous-looking tomes.

Ham took, from the top of a bookcase, a bit of fabric which looked as if it had been torn from the floor carpet of a car.

HAM waved the piece of carpet.

"A schoolboy brought this," he explained. "He said he'd found it lying on a road in New Jersey."

Doc Savage took the piece of carpet. Fastened to the underside by the clip which must have originally secured it to a ribbon, was a monocle.

"The boy said the monocle was wrapped in the piece of carpet so that it would not break," Ham explained.

"The monocle is Johnny's," Doc Savage said.

"It certainly is!"

The monocle was an elaborate one. The concave side of the frame was engraved with what, from a distance of a few feet, looked like ornamental scroll-work, but on closer examination this proved to be lettering:

$50 REWARD FOR RETURN OF THIS
TO DOC SAVAGE

"Johnny has all his monocles engraved that way, in case they get lost," Ham reminded. "Something has happened to him!"

"Obviously!" the bronze man agreed.

Ham shook his head slowly. "I'm afraid it won't help us much. Poor Johnny must have dropped it as a clue to indicate which way he was being taken. But it was dropped hours ago, and there are hundreds of roads in New Jersey. No telling where he is!"

Doc Savage said, "Suppose we examine the thing a bit more closely."

Wonderingly, Ham followed Doc into the laboratory. This was an enormous room, by far the largest in the establishment. It contained an incredible array of scientific equipment. The bottles and phials of chemicals must have numbered into thousands. There were supplies of rare metals. There were retorts, furnaces, even lathes for working metal, and a complete equipment of tools. It was here that Doc Savage developed and constructed a great many of his unusual devices.

From a cabinet, the bronze man produced a contrivance which resembled an old-fashioned magic lantern, except that the lens, although it resembled glass, was almost jet-black. Doc Savage pulled the shades, plugged the apparatus into an electric outlet and switched it on. He pointed it at Johnny's monocle.

The unexpected happened. Tiny, carefully made letters, previously invisible, appeared on the monocle's glass:

Seized. Blue taxie. Hole in top.

"Jove!" exploded Ham. "Johnny used some of that invisible chalk which is only brought out by ultra-violet light."

"The metal caps of his shoe laces hold some of the stuff," Doc Savage agreed. "He must have gotten the opportunity to pull the cap off a shoe lace and write this message."

"We'd better start hunting Johnny!"

"First, it might be wise to do some checking," Doc said, quietly.

"I don't get you."

"We are going to telephone a number of Wall Street brokerage houses."

"But what earthly good will that do?"

Doc Savage did not explain.

THE bronze man went back to the reception room and picked up the telephone book. He handed this to Ham.

"List names and telephone numbers of stock brokers," he directed.

Plainly not understanding the purpose behind the request Ham, nevertheless, complied. As soon as the first name and number was on paper, Doc Savage began telephoning. To each brokerage office, he put the same request.

"Give me the names of your customers who have made killings on the stock exchange recently?"

His average of answers was not much more than fifty per cent. Some brokers declared they would not answer such a question without a court order, even after Doc Savage explained his identity. Others declared it would take time to assemble such a list. But about half had the information available, and were familiar enough with Doc Savage's reputation to comply with his request. Doc listened intently to each recital of names. He did not write them down. His trained memory made that unnecessary, especially since he was only listening for the appearance of one particular name on more than one list.

He spent almost an hour telephoning, then put the instrument down for the last time.

His weird trilling note came into existence, persisted for the briefest of moments, then ebbed away into nothingness. Ham brightened. He had heard the sound often enough to know that it presaged an important discovery.

"You dug up something?" he asked.

"Market killings have not been very frequent recently in

Wall Street," Doc said. "Only one person seems to have taken a good deal of money out of Wall Street recently."

"Who?"

"Sylvan Niles," Doc Savage said.

"Who is Sylvan Niles?" Ham queried, looking puzzled.

Ham had not been enlightened about recent events. Doc now furnished him with the story, beginning with his own decision to investigate the Jethro Mandebran twenty-million-dollar disappearance.

In the midst of the recital, Ham walked to a chair on which reposed a cane, gloves, and a hat. He picked up the cane. It was a neat black stick. He stood fingering this through the remainder of the story.

Once, he twisted the handle slightly, and the stick came apart, disclosing that it was a sword cane with a blade of excellent steel.

Ham eyed Doc intently. "Have you any idea what's behind it?"

Doc Savage held his silence.

"It's bally sinister, whatever it is!" added Ham who, at times, affected an English accent.

UNFORTUNATELY, Ham was not gifted with an extra faculty which would enable him to look through thicknesses of plaster, steel and wood. Had he been able to do this, his hair might possibly have stood on end, although his hair was not addicted to demonstrations in the face of fear.

Doc Savage's office occupied the eighty-sixth floor of the skyscraper.

The eighty-fifth floor, the one immediately below Doc's headquarters, had been rented only the day before. The four renters were in the suite. Three held machine guns. These rapid-firers were of a foreign manufacture, evidence that Federal laws stopping the distribution from American makers was having an effect in crookdom. They were hungry, mean-looking fellows who had apparently led a hard life.

The fourth man was engaged in an extraordinary occupation. He was seated between two huge suitcases on the floor of the inner room. The bags were open and disclosed a complex assortment of apparatus, much of which seemed to be electrical in nature.

More interesting, however, was the unique headgear which the man wore. This piece of equipment gave the impression of a great amount of intricate apparatus packed into the smallest possible space. Quite a number of wires ran from it to the suitcases. Another wire ran into the adjacent room and extended up to the ceiling.

The man took off the headset. He had an ugly face, and he seemed angry.

"You, out there," he snarled at one of the gunners in the outer office.

"Yeah?"

"So you'd like to croak the bronze guy, huh?" snarled the first.

The gunners looked vastly startled.

"For the love of Pete, how'd you know—" The one gunner did not finish. He seemed to remember something. A silent laugh shook his frame.

"Ain't it a great world?" he grinned.

The man using the set was not amused. "Get the hell outta there!" he gritted. "You're mussing up things. Get over by the door!"

They hastily complied with the order. "You learnin' anything?" one called.

"Pipe down!" another of the machine gunners suggested. "You might be heard upstairs!"

"Not a chance!" said the first. "The bronze guy's place is darn near soundproof, I've heard."

The man with the headset had replaced that weird contrivance on his head. It covered his cranium completely, and lent him a grotesque appearance.

There was utter silence in the room for a number of minutes. Then the man suddenly wrenched the set off his head. Utter horror was on his face.

"The bronze guy!" he exploded. "He's got our whole layout figured!"

"He can't have!" gasped one of the guards.

"He has! He even knows who the boss is!"

Chapter X

FLIGHT

IN the reception room upstairs Ham, the dapper lawyer, was moving his head slowly, and sheathing and unsheathing his sword cane in a baffled way.

"What is behind it?" he was asking Doc Savage, for perhaps the fifth time.

The bronze man seemed to have gone suddenly deaf. He appeared not to hear the lawyer's question. He had offered no explanations of any theories that he held. Ham, as a matter of truth, was not surprised. He knew Doc. The bronze man was not often involved in a mystery for long before he had formulated some fairly correct convictions. But Doc was not in the habit of voicing suspicions which he was, for the time being, unable to prove, or which, for other reasons, he did not wish to divulge.

"Ham," Doc Savage said, suddenly, "we had best search this office."

"What?" Ham was open mouthed. "You think—"

"A suspicion has occurred to me," said Doc Savage. "Let us make sure."

The bronze man now led the way through the library to the laboratory. While three walls of this great room were inclosed mostly in windows, the fourth wall looked solid. This was deceptive, however, as Doc proved by manipulating concealed locks in a panel. The wall opened, disclosing an array of recording instruments. These consisted of clockwork devices that turned a paper disk on which an inked needle was dragged. One of the disks showed a line which had an irregularity in it. Doc pointed to this.

"Some three hours ago, a prowler entered through the reception room window. He must have gained the roof and lowered himself down. Considering the height of this building, he could have done that without being observed from the street."

"Any one observing him, would have thought him a window washer," Ham agreed. "Do you think he's hiding in here?"

Doc Savage pointed out a second wavy section in the recorded line. This inking device was connected to a clock, for the purpose of designating the exact time of a depredation. There was a recorder for each window and door.

"The man was inside for perhaps an hour," Doc Savage pointed out. "Then he left."

"We'd better see what he was up to," Ham growled.

"Exactly."

The bronze man now moved through his establishment, metallic eyes alert. He scrutinized various drawers and cabinet doors, all equipped with tiny hidden mechanisms which told whether or not the doors and drawers had been opened.

"The place was not searched," Doc Savage said.

"Then what would anybody break in for?"

"There can be only one reason."

"Yes?"

"Something was planted here!"

There was a *pow!* of a noise, and a great sheet of flame lashed before their eyes.

Doc Savage grasped dapper Ham and yanked him bodily backward, which probably saved him. It was a chair, one of the large overstuffed ones, which had literally exploded. The blast, however, had not been nearly as violent as the one downtown in the office of the Castello Mining Corporation.

The bursting did throw streams of what looked like superheated liquid fire. Some of this splashed almost where Doc and Ham had been standing, but by that time the two men were back in the laboratory, sheltered to one side of the door.

Wherever the liquid fire splashes struck, there was a burst of flame. The heat was blistering, terrific. Even Habeas, the pig, tough though his hide was, had backed into a corner for safety.

After the incendiary chemical had fallen, they made an attempt to get through the office to the door. It was impossible, due to the heat.

Doc and Ham retreated. The bronze man opened a panel and wrenched one of three levers. There was a loud hissing noise in the reception room. From concealed vents along the molding came streams of chemical which vaporized as it settled downward. This was the fire extinguishing system which Doc Savage himself had installed. The flames, hot as they were, began to subside.

But the chair, its contents—whatever they were—had been destroyed.

"What set that stuff off?" Ham yelled.

"Men in an office below," Doc Savage decided, quietly.

"I'll look into that!" Ham growled, and dashed for the laboratory.

Although there was apparently no means of exit from Doc's establishment other than the conventional door through the reception room, it was actually possible to step from the laboratory through a concealed panel into the corridor. Ham passed through this secret exit in great haste, picking up a rapid-firing machine pistol on the way. The rapid-firer shot anæsthetic mercy bullets that did not kill—one of Doc Savage's inventions.

At the end of the hallway, stairs descended. Ham clattered down. He had completed half his descent when a gun slammed lead at him from below.

Ham grunted. It was a very loud, pained grunt. He sat down heavily on the stairs. Involuntarily, he clasped both hands over his middle.

The bullet had hit him squarely in the stomach!

HAM's head swam. Awful lights jumped in his eyeballs. As a matter of fact, he had just received the equivalent of a terrific solar plexus blow. He began to feel quite ill.

But he breathed brief and silent thanks for a bulletproof undergarment, which all of Doc Savage's aids habitually wore. The protector was of chain mail, woven from a specially developed alloy of extreme strength. It was light and stopped bullets, although the shock was sometimes sufficient to break bones and leave rather terrible bruises.

The gun below crashed again. The bullet missed, partially because Ham heaved up and retreated.

He got a brief glimpse of the person trying to kill him. It was a lean, soured-looking man whose pinched face, while it had nothing definitely wrong with it, was not a prepossessing visage. The man was using a revolver which appeared to be of foreign manufacture.

Ham coughed several times and rubbed his midriff. He had retained his grip on the machine pistol. Now he leveled it.

The gun made a noise like the moan of a bullfiddle magnified many times.

The gunman who had fired the shot was no longer in sight, so Ham had no definite target. He was shooting for effect. He knew how unnerving was the great noise of the superfirer.

There was no return fire. Ham scuttled down the stairs, gingerly. The bullet against his stomach had knocked caution into him.

He ran into the corridor and peered at the line of elevator cages. One of these seemed to have just started down. Wheeling, he dashed back up the stairway and into the corridor of the floor which housed Doc Savage's quarters.

"Doc!" Ham squalled.

"Yes?"

"They're taking an elevator down!" Ham screeched. "I'm going to follow in the speed lift!"

"No!" Doc Savage called, sharply.

Ham howled, "They'll get away!"

"Did you give them a scare?" Doc Savage demanded.

"I don't know about that," Ham said. "But they gave me one!"

"They're leaving, though?"

"Oh, yes."

"Come in here."

Puzzled, Ham entered the laboratory by the secret panel which he had left open—to discover Doc Savage leaning through a window.

In Doc's hand was a rifle with a barrel almost as large as that of a shotgun.

Where the bronze man stood, he could see the building entrance far below. Even as Ham came up, Doc reached into a cabinet, secured a pair of binoculars and focused them on the sidewalk, as an aid to identifying any one who appeared.

"You do the same," he told Ham.

The dapper lawyer hurriedly complied, at the same time using one hand to rub his stomach, which was still troubling him. Ham watched the sidewalk closely. His glasses were powerful.

Four men soon came out of the building far below.

"There they are," Ham said.

The four men walked directly to a large car which was parked at the curb. They entered.

"They're going to get away!" Ham groaned.

Doc Savage's reply was to lift the rifle very deliberately and fire. The noise of the gun was much less than might have been anticipated. It was not much more than a loud cough.

HAM leaned out of the window with his glasses, staring. He saw the car swing away from the curb as if nothing had happened. The rifle in Doc Savage's hands made its strange soft cough again. The car below did not falter in its flight. It rolled rapidly.

"You're missing it!" Ham gasped, incredulously. The lawyer knew that the bronze man, although he rarely resorted to the use of firearms, was an expert shot.

The fugitives' car disappeared around a corner.

"Gone!" Ham yelped.

"Come on!" Doc Savage clipped.

The bronze man made a swift dash for the reception room and looked over the scene there. The fire had been extinguished completely. He leaped to the ruins of the chair, made a brief scrutiny. There was nothing to be found. Destruction had been complete.

"There must have been something in that chair!" Ham gasped.

"There was," Doc Savage told him. "But they were too quick for us. They destroyed it."

Back into the laboratory, Doc raced, Ham at his heels. The bronze man opened a hidden panel, one which Ham had not touched in his passage to the hall. This one gave admission to a bullet-shaped cage, the interior of which was padded and equipped with straps for hanging on. The thing was not large. They dived inside it. Ham had scooped up Monk's pig and taken it along, much as he despised the porker.

Doc closed the hatches of the bullet-like car, and touched a lever. The results were astounding. There was a loud moan of compressed air and machinery. The car sank like a plummet. A few moments later, there was a violent wrench as the car changed its course. It was like a pea being shot through the barrel of a blowgun. The noise was ear-splitting. Conversation was impossible. Then the effects of braking mechanism could be felt. The car slowed. With a clank, it stopped, and Doc Savage opened the hatch. They stepped out.

A few seconds before, they had been on the top floor of the skyscraper, but their surroundings now were vastly different. It was a huge building of brick, of steel—Doc Savage's water-front airplane hangar and boathouse.

This hangar was as much a secret as it was possible to keep it. Outer appearance of the building differed little from other water-front structures, being a huge edifice of grimy brick. It was erected on a pier. Across the front a sign said simply:

HIDALGO TRADING COMPANY

The Hidalgo Trading Company was Doc Savage.

The big building housed a number of planes, boats, a small dirigible, and even a submarine.

Doc Savage chose a small amphibian gyroplane—a windmill ship which was perfect for work at close quarters.

Ham, in the meantime, seemed to have something else on his mind.

"Chemistry!" Ham called loudly. "Chemistry!"

A CREATURE of astounding physical appearance waddled into view—astounding because the physical likeness which the animal bore to the homely chemist, Monk, was a bit uncanny. Chemistry was a large, tailless monkey with a certain number of human points—just enough of them, in fact, to make it possible for him to be mistaken for Monk, if seen at a distance and in somewhat inadequate light.

"Come on, Chemistry!" Ham called.

Chemistry swung into the gyro. Ham boosted the pig in next.

Chemistry was Ham's pet, one he had lately acquired as a defensive organism against Monk's pet pig, Habeas Corpus. Chemistry and Habeas got along together practically as well as did Ham and Monk—which meant they never quite got to the point of slaughtering each other.

Doc Savage started the gyro motor, and the ship rolled down the incline and intercepted light beams which played on a photo-electric cell, causing the hangar doors to open. The doors closed automatically as soon as the plane was out on the river.

Shortly, the ship was in the air.

Chapter XI

QUEER MEN

THE gyro cabin was soundproof, although not perfectly so. The engine, an air-cooled radial, fed its exhaust gasses through a valve which directed them either into a long silencing cylinder, or into the open air. During takeoff, the cutouts were open, noisy. Doc closed them when they were in the air, to permit conversation.

"Get the fluoroscopic spectacle devices," Doc Savage directed Ham.

The dapper lawyer moved into the rear of the plane cabin, probed into special lockers, and came out with two contrivances which bore a very faint resemblance to goggles. At least, they fitted over the eyes, goggle-fashion. The lenses, however, were as large as condensed milk cans and were very black.

Ham moved a tiny lever on the sides of the canlike lenses. They began to make the same kind of sounds given off by a miniature motion-picture camera when in operation. Ham fitted the lenses over his eyes.

The bronze man manipulated the plane's controls. Soon they flew over the masonry canyons that were the streets of uptown New York.

Ham leaned from the window, peering downward through his strange eyegear. He could distinguish only the faintest outlines of what was below.

"Watch for what looks like a brighter patch of light," Doc Savage directed.

"Righto," Ham agreed. "I know now what we're looking for."

Ham watched the terrain below intently.

"There it is!" he called.

Immediately, the bronze man sent the gyro up.

"Watch the car!" Doc Savage warned.

The gyro climbed and climbed. Ham paid no attention to

that. He knew Doc was getting up where they would not attract notice. Planes are plentiful over New York, and the conventional autogyros are not uncommon. This ship, although it was true gyro, could hardly be distinguished from an autogyro at a distance.

Ham kept a close watch on the spot of light. It was fading, but still discernible.

The lawyer knew what it was. It was the top of the car in which the men had escaped.

Doc Savage had fired his unusual-looking gun at the machine. The purpose of this had puzzled Ham for a time. The bullets had been shells containing a chemical concoction in liquefied state, which had splashed on the car roof. This stuff had made a film, perhaps unnoticeable to the naked eye, which reflected infra light better than the surroundings. This was doing with infra light what a film does with ordinary light.

Doc Savage had merely arranged to trail the quarry to their hangout, hoping thereby to find Johnny or Monk.

THE State of New Jersey has an unusual distribution of inhabitants. Directly across the Hudson River from New York City and a bit to the southwest, is Newark, a metropolis, a city of consequence. Not a great many miles distant, however, are sections of brush-covered hill country which might almost be called uninhabited.

It was into this isolated section that the trail Doc Savage was following led. The bronze man was flying the gyro high, and Ham was employing binoculars to keep track of the car below.

"The car is pulling into a farm!" Ham called, abruptly.

Doc Savage took the binoculars for a moment. They were fully twice as long as the largest ordinary field glasses, and their magnifying power was a good deal more than twice as great. They had, in fact, the strength of a small celestial telescope.

The bronze man studied the spot where the quarry had stopped. There was a high stone wall and a house, a great rambling thing of wood. The structure was of a style popular fifty years ago.

One car already stood in the yard. From Doc's height, it was impossible to tell with certainty, but the machine appeared to be a taxicab, painted a faded blue color.

There was a small hole—it might have been made by a man's head thrusting upward hard—in the top of the cab.

"Hope Johnny and his big words haven't come to harm," Ham said, slowly.

Doc Savage piloted the gyro in a wide swing, until the craft was in the sky directly west of the house to which their quarry had gone. To see the plane now, any one at the house would have to look almost directly into the afternoon sun. Even then, it was highly unlikely that the ship could be discerned.

"You take the plane off again," Doc Savage directed Ham.

"Righto!" agreed Ham, not looking particularly pleased with the assignment.

"If either of the cars leave, follow them."

Doc landed the gyro in a small clearing. Ham got the ship back in the air immediately, and Doc struck out through the scrubby hill growth.

When Doc got close to the huge, ancient wooden house and its imposing stone wall, he used more caution and searched for a posted guard. His scrutiny of the brush, the ground, was infinitely painstaking. Particularly did he examine the sheer threads of cobwebs, on the theory that one of these could be fine wire, the breaking of which might set a bell ringing.

The wall around the house, in the rear, was coated with ivy vines. This foliage was thick and green.

Doc Savage scrutinized the place intently. The upper parts of the house which he could see, looked decrepit, deserted. There was no sound, no movement.

Doc's pockets were rather amply filled with various of his innumerable gadgets, and he now produced one of these somewhat the shape and size of a cigar case. He opened this.

It proved to hold some apparatus and a small, watchcase receiver. He placed the receiver to an ear, then turned the apparatus slowly, as he would a searchlight.

The thing was an amplifier and sound pick-up, tiny but remarkably sensitive. It could catch the buzzing of a fly, for instance, farther away than the fly could be seen with the naked eye. Whatever the bronze man heard, it seemed to be interesting.

He exchanged the listener gadget for another device about three times the size of the little boxes which hold ordinary pocket matches. This container was of metal. The top had a saucerlike depression, and there were various dials on the sides.

Doc Savage placed this contrivance in the shrubbery. He left it there and walked forward. Something like a score of paces brought him within a dozen feet of the wall.

The vines covering the wall parted and a man stepped out with a sawed off shotgun, cocked.

"Howdy," said the man.

Doc Savage stood perfectly still, and replied nothing.

"Mister, maybe you think we ain't glad to see you!" The man leered. "Bend over and take hold of the toes of your shoes with both hands, and stand like that."

Doc Savage complied with the command. It put him at a distinct disadvantage. The other advanced warily.

"I've heard a lot about you, big guy," he growled. "I ain't takin' no chances."

He pressed his gun to Doc's back with his right hand, and with his left began slapping spots where there was likely to be a holstered weapon. He was as worried as a green lion tamer on his first job. It showed in his manner. However, he took no chances.

Before long, something happened which disrupted proceedings. Out of the brush behind them came a voice, shrill, distinctly metallic. It was not a calm or natural voice, but then no voice could be expected to be calm, under the circumstances.

"Drop that shotgun!" ordered the voice.

It was inevitable that the man with the shotgun would look up to make sure the new speaker meant business. When he did this, Doc grabbed the fellow's ankles and yanked. The man upset. His gun did not go off, due to Doc's quickness in clamping on his wrist a grip which caused the finger sinews to slacken rather than tighten. The struggle which ensued was terrific, but lasted not much longer than it would have taken a man to get a long breath.

Having flattened the man on his back, holding him with throat clamped so no noise could escape, Doc Savage caused unconsciousness by exerting his specialized pressure on spinal nerve centers. This was as effective as a knockout blow, and not noisy.

THE moment the victim was senseless, Doc Savage retreated hastily into the brush and picked up the metal contrivance which he had placed there before advancing. It was still giving forth an almost inaudible whirring noise and would, in the course of a few seconds, repeat other commands to surrender. There was a tiny record inside, and the concave area in the top of the box was simply a reproducer diaphragm. Doc Savage shut the thing off, pocketed it and went back to the prisoner.

The fellow had not stirred and would not for at least an hour to come. Doc Savage picked him up and carried him to a niche in the wall which was concealed by vines. The niche proved to be perhaps about three feet in depth, the same in width and high enough for even Doc Savage to stand erect.

While the wall around the house was manifestly very old, this niche seemed to have been constructed more recently, within the past few weeks, judging from the appearance of the mortar. The rear was a wooden door—unlocked, fortunately.

There was a square opening in the door, not quite a foot across, and this was strapped with iron bars. Doc Savage looked through the aperture.

The old house looked even larger than it had from a distance. The ramshackle aspect seemed to have increased somewhat. It could be noted, however, that the shingles were intact on the roof, and that, while the shutters were, in some cases, loose and even hanging by as little as a single hinge, the windows were all unbroken. Moreover, none of the siding was loose. As a matter of fact, the house was in good condition, except for paint and minor repairs.

There was shrubbery in the yard, beds planted irregularly in the old-fashioned way. Lawn grass was uncut. Such paths as were in the yard were constructed of processions of large, flat stones, and close inspection disclosed they had received recent use.

The bronze man crawled swiftly, making little noise. About the house was the silence of a tomb. Basement windows seemed to offer a means of entry. Doc Savage headed for them.

The bronze man learned later that the grounds were wired with an extremely modern type of burglar alarm. The wires of the contraption were buried underground, and the effect as he passed over them caused sensitive relays to set off an indicator.

The first hint of this was the appearance of movement in one of the upstairs windows. Some one was behind the window, staring downward. The individual moved closer to the pane, the glass of which had been washed recently.

It was the girl, Sylvan Niles!

SHE apparently saw Doc Savage. Then she was gone from sight. The next instant, there was a crashing noise. Glass dropped out of the window where the girl had been. A bullet bedded viciously alongside Doc Savage.

The bronze man moved. Most of his torso was incased in a bulletproof garment of chain mail, but his head and neck were always vulnerable to a well-aimed or a lucky shot. Out of his coat he drew a metal egg. There was a small lever on the side of this. He flicked the lever, and threw the small spheroid close to the side of the house.

The thing hatched with a flash that hurt the eyes and a roar that menaced eardrums. A portion of the house wall fell inward. Glass jumped out of windows all along the side of the house. There was some bluish-looking smoke and a not inconsiderable quantity of dust.

And there was a hole in the side of the house through which a horse, providing he was agile, might have jumped.

Chapter XII

THE BURDEN OF SUSPICION

DOC SAVAGE was in motion. He calculated nicely, allowing just enough time for flying débris to settle, but moving quickly enough that the dust and smoke would help conceal him.

A mess of splintered laths and torn flooring delayed him slightly. The wreckage was still groaning as it settled. A large scab of plaster fell tardily off the ceiling.

Doc waded over the torn mass of a rug, sidestepped a divan which the explosion had mangled. There was a mirror door and an ordinary door side by side at the end of the room. Most of the mirror glass was out. Being aware that mirrors are usually put in closet doors, Doc Savage ignored that one. The second panel was stuck. It proved simpler to bash the thin wood out and crawl through, than to bother with opening it.

A gun barked at him the instant he was in a hall. He rolled, twisted, and gained an angle in the corridor. Where he had been when the shot crashed, a cloud of black smoke appeared. It spread rapidly. A draft pulled some of it through the hole which he had smashed in the door. The rest mushroomed out in the hallway, shutting off visibility.

The stuff was coming from a metal container which Doc had left there.

The gun did not slam again. The shot had come from a point which seemed to be a staircase. Up this, feet pattered. The noise they made was rapid and rather light, almost effeminate.

Doc Savage headed toward the fleeing individual. The smoke, while it concealed him completely when he was within the cloud, left no traces of soot on his person. Nor did he seem to have difficulty breathing while in it. However, creeping toward the stairs, he fell to absently rubbing his hands, one with the other. He rubbed his neck. Then, apparently realizing what he was doing, he put forth an effort and stopped this.

That smoke bomb was a very particular type. A great deal of experimenting had gone into its concoction.

At the foot of the stairway, he paused.

"Johnny!" he called.

"Here!" came a muffled voice.

It was Johnny's voice, although the wordy archæologist and geologist rarely used a word so small. He seemed to be upstairs and toward the front of the house.

Bullets came down the staircase in a businesslike procession. It was plain that whoever was up there wanted to be alone with the prisoner.

Doc Savage produced another of the powerful little grenades.

"You had better move!" he called to the gunman. "In about ten seconds, there is not going to be much left of the spot where you are standing!"

The bronze man listened intently. He never killed or seriously injured any one, if it could be avoided.

The bullets kept coming.

Doc adjusted the firing mechanism of the grenade. He chose a moment when there was a pause in the shooting and flicked the little thing upward. It landed with a small clatter.

The gunman fled.

The house shook on its foundations. Noise, smoke, laths, plaster, and a few stray stair treads came flying down. In the spot where Doc crouched, plaster fell off the ceiling and deluged him painfully.

He went up the stairway. The hall above was a wreck. A door at the end had been pretty well demolished.

The girl, Sylvan Niles, lay just beyond it. She was on her face, senseless, and it looked as if something had hit her on the back of the head. Fragments of the door were scattered over most of the room. Her outflung right hand still held a revolver.

Doc SAVAGE lunged to the young woman, dropped beside her, and proceeded to demonstrate that a man can simultaneously do an entirely different thing with each hand. With his left hand, he felt the girl's pulse and learned she was alive, then turned her head and opened her eyes. He moved her head, holding her eyes open. The inactivity of her eyeballs during this operation proved that she was genuinely senseless.

With his right hand, the bronze man opened the revolver. It was the type which held five cartridges, and all had been discharged. The fact that the barrel was warm proved the firing had been recent.

Doc Savage closed the revolver and replaced it in her hand exactly as he had found it.

Heaving erect, the bronze man lunged across the room and found what had evidently, in the heyday of the old mansion, been a serving pantry. From this, a stairway led down.

He listened. Men were leaving the house; several of them, judging from the noise. They seemed to be getting into the cars. Doc did not move to descend the stairs. They would be expecting that. He found a door admitting to that side of the house where the automobiles stood. He tried it. Locked. He lunged against it. With a tearing of wood, it came open.

In the center of the room stood a strange-looking thing. It was longer, higher, wider than a man. A box. But the wood looked very ancient, and on it were limned cabalistic symbols in vermilion and purple and gold.

Any young lad moderately up on his history could have identified the thing. A mummy case!

Small, weird sounds were coming out of the case.

Doc Savage ignored the noises. He flung to a window, tried to get it up, and found it was nailed in place. He smashed the glass out of one panel.

He did not put his head through, for the very excellent reason that a swarm of bullets arrived. The slugs took the remainder of the glass out and made a great noise against the ceiling. Other pellets began clouting through the walls of the house itself. These last must have been the product of high-powered rifles. A machine gun of some light variety using revolver cartridges was playing through the window.

The motors of two automobiles could be heard through this battle uproar.

DOC SAVAGE veered to the left, at the same time producing another grenade. He did not often make a gesture which he knew in advance would be futile, but he made one now. He flung the grenade, knowing very well, from the angle at which he had to throw it, that the thing would land nowhere near the cars. The concussion, however, might be morally effective on the occupants of the machines.

The roar was tremendous, and the whole house shook. Immediately, the shooting stopped. The cars went away, motors straining for speed.

The noises were still coming from the mummy case.

Doc Savage took a chance and leaned from the window. Two cars—the taxi-cab with the hole in the top and the vehicle which Doc and Ham had trailed to the spot—were on the road. From the way they were bouncing, the occupants must have been having a rough time. The road was not fit for speed such as they were making.

Doc went to the mummy case. His swift scrutiny showed him that it was undoubtedly genuine. Mummies are not technically supposed to arise from their receptacles, and the ancients had taboos against outsiders desecrating the contents of such cases. Therefore, it was not equipped with a lock. But some one had fastened the lid down by the simple expedient of tying a rope around the whole case.

Doc Savage untied the rope and opened the lid.

The long, bony man inside sat up and gulped, "I'll be super-amalgamated!"

WILLIAM HARPER LITTLEJOHN had, at one time, taught in a college. Right now he looked anything but a professor. The only thing he wore was a breechcloth which he had fashioned of a large towel. His hair was down in his eyes, and he was dirt and bruises and dried blood from head to foot.

"I'll be superamalgamated!" he gulped again, and left the mummy case as if it were the last place in the world where he wanted to be.

"You all right?" Doc Savage asked.

"Do I look like I'm all right?" Johnny demanded, indignantly. "The answer is, no! Emphatically, no!"

He was all right.

"An unequivocal, baleful demoniacality!" he sputtered.

Doc Savage looked at the sarcophagus. While not absolutely airtight, it was nearly so.

"You were not in there long," he said, stating an obvious fact.

"No," Johnny agreed. "I heard you call and answered. They grabbed me, slammed me in there and roped the lid shut. Blast their souls! I might have smothered!"

Johnny, while he affected big words in the course of ordinary conversation, was not exclusively addicted to them. He did not, as a usual thing, employ his big words in the presence of Doc Savage. Rather, he used them to confound lesser listeners.

"Did they torture you much?" Doc Savage asked.

"I should say they did!"

"Trying to learn what?"

"They were endeavoring to ascertain just how much you knew of this whole devilish mystery," Johnny explained. "In doing that, they were, of course, butting their heads against a stone wall. Not that I like to designate myself as a stone wall. Quite the contrary. I think I proved very invulnerable."

"How much did you tell them?"

"All I knew," announced Johnny. "It amounted to exactly nothing, so I could see no harm in telling them."

"They did not believe you?"

"Naturally not. Hence, their playful parading back and forth across my chest. They also kicked me, pulled some of my hair out, and were getting around to throwing lighted matches at my eyes when you arrived."

DOC SAVAGE nodded. He seemed to be interested in the sarcophagus. He moved it. There was a round hole perhaps two inches across bored in the floor directly beneath the coffin. There was nothing in the hole.

Doc Savage examined the bottom of the sarcophagus and found another hole, a bit larger than the one in the floor, in the bottom of the death box. He peered into this. It was too dark to see anything.

"Did they talk much?" the bronze man asked.

"Too much!" said Johnny. "They talked all of the time. They were very windy."

"They dropped hints?"

"No man, or group of men, can talk as much as they did without dropping hints!"

Doc Savage was scrutinizing the inside of the sarcophagus. It seemed to be solid. He produced a pocketknife and scraped. This revealed that the box, sometime in the recent past, had been taken apart. He continued scraping until he located the joints.

"How many in the gang which held you?"

"I can't say," said Johnny. "Quite a number. They came and went."

"A dozen?"

"At least that many."

Doc Savage seated himself on one side of the open sarcophagus, put his feet against the other side. He prepared to use strength.

"Hear anything of Monk?" he asked.

"Have they got Monk?" Johnny exploded.

"Yes."

"I'll be superamalgamated!" groaned Johnny.

THE bronze man put forth a little exertion. The sarcophagus cracked, but did not give. He changed his position to use more advantageously his great strength.

"I didn't hear a word about Monk," Johnny said, grimly.

"We've got to find him," Doc Savage said. "That is our first job."

Johnny nodded. He moistened his lips. Then, because there seemed nothing else to comment upon, he pointed at the mummy case.

"There is something queer about that thing," he said. "I have suspected before this that my brain is not the greatest in the world. But now I have a suspicion that it is the dumbest!

They put me in that case several times, then took me out again and took me into another room. I could not make heads nor tails of it."

Doc Savage exerted the power of his leg muscles suddenly, violently. There was a ripping, and the mummy case came apart. Doc turned it over and continued his wrecking until he had it entirely separated, the entrails of the thing exposed.

Johnny peered with great interest. He bent down and stared. If there had been a fly speck present, he would have found it.

"Somebody," he gulped, "is crazy!"

The bottom of the mummy case and a considerable portion of the sides were hollow, but contained nothing.

"Were you in this room all the time," Doc Savage asked.

"No." Johnny frowned. "They could have taken something out of that without me seeing."

"They did," Doc Savage told him.

"Eh?" Johnny frowned at the bronze man. "You've got an idea of what this is all about?"

Instead of relieving the lank archæologist-geologist's mind, Doc Savage gestured. "There is a person down the hall whom you might be interested in seeing."

Johnny nodded, started for the door, then stopped.

"I forgot to tell you something," he said—"the name of their chief."

"You heard that?"

"Oh, yes. They seemed quite certain I was not going to leave here alive, so the name was mentioned."

"What was the name?"

"Sylvan Niles. A very bloodthirsty fellow, this Sylvan Niles, I take it!"

The bronze man escorted the battered Johnny to the spot where the young woman lay unconscious. He pointed.

"Sylvan Niles," he said.

"A woman!" Johnny gulped. "I'll be superamalgamated!"

Doc Savage asked, "You are sure that the leader of this gang is named Sylvan Niles?"

"That is what their conversation led me to believe," Johnny reiterated.

SYLVAN NILES showed no signs of consciousness returning immediately.

"Wait here," Doc Savage directed.

The bronze man made a thorough search of the place. Particularly did he scrutinize the room below the sarcophagus. The hole was prominent in the ceiling. It seemed to come straight through. Plaster which had fallen off the ceiling littered the floor. Doc Savage pushed this to one side with a toe and examined the floor. He found nothing there to interest him, and continued his search of the house.

Evidently the place had been used as a living quarters, but for an interval of no longer than a week or so. This was indicated by the state of the discarded cans which had held food. Some cans had not been cleaned out thoroughly, so that it was possible to form an estimate.

It became apparent that there was no one else in the house.

Doc Savage stepped out into the yard at the rear, where he had left the man he had overcome; but that fellow was gone. He had been in no condition to navigate under his own power, so it followed logically that some of his friends, in their flight, had gathered him up and carried him away.

Doc went back upstairs.

WILLIAM HARPER LITTLEJOHN was surveying senseless Sylvan Niles with a great deal of interest. Johnny cut quite an impressive figure in his breechcloth.

"There are window draperies downstairs," Doc Savage suggested. "They might make a more fitting garment than that towel. Your clothing seems to have disappeared."

"Good night!" Johnny exclaimed. "I had entirely forgotten."

Johnny hurried out, treading gingerly over broken plaster and splintered wood, and worked his way down the stairs. He came back some minutes later, arrayed in a crude toga which he had fashioned out of window draperies. His pipestem legs and arms protruded from this, giving the somewhat unearthly impression that he was composed exclusively of bones.

Doc Savage had opened the window and was leaning far out of it. Johnny noted that the bronze man seemed to scrutinize the sky.

"Something up there?" he asked.

"Ham was supposed to be flying around in the gyro," Doc replied. "He seems to have disappeared."

At this point, Sylvan Niles turned slightly and made a sighing sound. After an interval, she had her eyes open and was sitting up.

She said nothing. She simply looked at Doc Savage, and then at Johnny. She blinked several times when she saw Johnny, as if his grotesque figure were something new in her experience.

When Johnny would have spoken, Doc Savage admonished silence with a slight gesture. They watched the young woman. She peered about and evidently decided where she was. She looked at the wreckage which the grenade had made, then started to feel the lump on her head, which must have been paining considerably. This gesture brought to her attention the revolver which she held in her hand.

She pointed the gun at Doc Savage and Johnny.

Johnny groaned, "Doc, we should have taken that away from her!"

"Stand still, you two!" the young woman rapped. "I'm going to get out of here!"

Instead of standing still, Doc Savage advanced. He came slowly, giving her ample opportunity to pull the trigger.

"Back!" Sylvan Niles gritted.

Doc came on. The young woman cocked the gun. She set herself desperately and put on what she evidently intended to look like a determined expression. But when Doc Savage was almost upon her, she threw the gun down.

"You've got too darn much faith in your ability to read human nature!" she snapped at Doc. "I *might* have shot!"

DOC SAVAGE neglected to inform her that the chance of her shooting him with a gun in which all of the cartridges had been discharged was negligible. He picked up the gun and tossed it out of the window.

"What happened to you?" Doc asked her.

She seemed to be a young woman who was coherent with her descriptions.

"You left me with Monk, young Alex Mandebran, and that pig, Habeas, in front of the Miners' Building," she said. "We had only been there a few moments, when a man came along knocked on the car window and said he had a message from you. Monk opened the door. The man managed to keep the door open while other men ran up. They grabbed us."

"They gagged and blindfolded you immediately?" Doc asked, remembering that he had seen her and young Alex Mandebran without either blindfold or gag in the departing car.

"No," she said. "They did that later."

"Then what?"

"They brought me here. They took Monk and Alex Mandebran somewhere else. I don't know where."

The vicious treatment he had received led Johnny to burst in with a suspicious question.

"Suppose you explain how you were left senseless with that gun in your hand?" he requested.

"They hit me on the head and left me that way!"

"That is at least a good story," Johnny said.

The girl glared angrily. "Who are you, you funny-looking bag of bones?"

Doc Savage supplied, "He is William Harper Littlejohn, more often known as Johnny, one of my aids."

"I am disappointed!" said the young woman. "It looks as if you went to the zoo for your assistants!"

JOHNNY favored the young woman with the coldest of stares, but did not address her again.

Doc Savage asked the girl, "Will you talk freely now?"

"No!"

"It might make matters simpler."

She shook her head mutely, then seemed to think of something. She pointed at the basement regions. "Did you search down there?"

"Hurriedly," Doc Savage admitted.

"They had a hide-out underneath," said the girl. "Some of them might have got in there. We'd better look."

Doc Savage helped her to her feet and it was evident that she could walk, although with some uncertainty. They negotiated the torn area at the top of the stairs and descended.

The basement was not large. The floor was of packed clay, the walls of ancient brick. Directly in the center, rising like a ponderous column, was the foundation of a fireplace, evidently in the room above. At the foot of this was a tiny door for the removal of ashes.

The girl pointed. "There."

Doc Savage opened the ash door and looked into the chimney foundation. He took a small stick and poked, bringing out nothing but soot.

"It's there," said the girl. "You step into the side of the chimney, or something."

Doc Savage searched. Whoever had made the recess had

done an excellent job. The joint was hardly perceptible, even with a magnifying glass. The mechanism which opened the thing defied discovery entirely. Doc went outside, got a heavy rock, came back and smashed it against the chimney.

In a moment, he had a panel uncovered—a panel as wide as his shoulders, almost as high as his head. It was of metal, and the brick had been cemented to the outside. Doc got it open.

The recess beyond would accommodate his person with some squeezing. The footing was not firm when he stepped upon it. There were ropes on the right hand side, indicating the thing was an elevator, operating in dumbwaiter fashion.

"Send the young lady down after me," Doc directed.

The bronze man turned in the lift, manipulated the ropes and without much noise, he sank. Several times, he put finger tips against the sides of the concrete shaft in order to estimate speed. The lift dropped nearly fifteen feet before coming to a stop. Doc produced a flashlight.

The walls were shored up with timbers. There was only a single room, and that not large. The place was equipped with a bench and innumerable boxes. Tools were scattered on the bench.

On the bench also was a high stack of papers. Doc Savage went over and scrutinized these. They were receipts for stocks bought and sold on the New York and other stock exchanges.

The name of the trader in each case was Sylvan Niles. Sylvan Niles seemed to be a financial wizard. In no case had money been lost; and the winnings, in some instances, amounted to many thousands of dollars.

Doc Savage went back to the shaft and called, "Send Sylvan Niles down!"

"Righto," called Johnny.

A MOMENT later, the lift, which Johnny had pulled up, descended and the young woman stepped out. Doc was holding a flashlight and he studied her features intently in its glow, as she looked the place over. Either she was genuinely surprised by her surroundings, or she was an excellent actress.

Then Johnny came down.

"Just exactly what is in this den?" he demanded, peering about.

"Some kind of mechanical construction has been carried

on here," Doc Savage said. "We might try to ascertain exactly what was built."

They centered attention on the boxes. They were already opened. Every box was entirely empty. Some still held excelsior packing. This was pulled out carefully and sifted, divulging nothing of interest. There was not even a scrap of paper. The boxes themselves bore no markings.

The two men went to the bench, scrutinized the tools. Doc indicated a long rack above the bench which, evidently, had once held a great many tools, but was now empty.

"Every clue has been disposed of," the bronze man said.

A shrill gasp drew their attention to Sylvan Niles. She had walked to the sheaf of buy-and-sell-order confirmations, and was examining them. She was agog.

"You made a nice profit!" the bronze man said, dryly.

"I?" she exploded. "I never saw these before!"

Johnny hurried over to the papers, cast a glance over them, then eyed the girl.

"Hermeneutical catachresis is expedient," he remarked.

"What?"

"Your explanation had better be good," Johnny told her.

"I've been framed!" she snapped. "Some one has been trading on the stock market and using my name!"

Johnny shook his head solemnly. "Very thin!"

Then, as if to go through the papers more thoroughly, Johnny picked up the whole bundle. The results were discomfiting. There was a loud grating of metal overhead, a clang. Doc Savage lunged to the shaft and looked upward.

A heavy steel plate had slid across the shaft, closing it. By wedging himself into the shaft, Doc climbed upward to the barrier and exerted his strength against it. The thing was entirely solid.

They were trapped!

JOHNNY was looking at the spot on the table where the papers had lain. Coming up through holes in the wood were two tiny wires, insulated except for the tips, which had been held together by the weight of the papers. Lifting the documents had allowed the wires to separate, breaking an electric circuit, which had, in turn, resulted in the closing of the shaft.

"A trap!"

The girl said nothing.

Johnny secured a stout screw driver, scrambled up in the shaft and worked on the trap panel, but made no noticeable progress toward getting it out of their way. Clinging in the shaft was a difficult business, and he dropped back to the floor shortly, exhausted.

"I'll be superamalgamated!" he mumbled. "We're in a jam sure enough now! We'll never get out of here!"

Chapter XIII

HAM HAS DIFFICULTIES

BRIGADIER GENERAL THEODORE MARLEY BROOKS was, at the moment, nowhere near the old country house where Doc, Johnny and Sylvan Niles were trapped. Furthermore, Ham was heading away from it, and hoping his gyro would not be seen by the occupants of the two cars traversing New Jersey highways at a high rate of speed.

In the rear of the plane, Ham's pet monkey, Chemistry, and Monk's pig, Habeas Corpus, quarreled. They were evenly matched. Habeas could bite, use his sharp-hoofed feet; Chemistry, while larger, had only monkey fists and less effective teeth.

Ham had little difficulty keeping track of his quarry, except when they passed through villages. Fortunately, there were no large towns.

The cars took to a disused woodland road. Boughs arched over this thoroughfare so that, at times, the machines were completely hidden from view. Ham resisted the temptation to fly lower, knowing it was quiet in the woodland and they might hear the noise of the plane's motor. His eyes ached intolerably from the strain of using binoculars.

Then a peculiar thing happened. The two cars pulled off the road into a tiny clearing which was surrounded by a dense wall of foliage. In this clearing stood two other cars. It was impossible to tell a great deal about these machines from this height, but they looked long, powerful. The men changed cars.

The dapper lawyer decided drivers had been waiting with a change of cars in the clearing.

The two relief machines headed back the way the others had come. They traveled at a high rate of speed, and because two fast cars, one behind the other, would tend to attract attention, they separated a distance of perhaps three quarters of a mile. These machines were much more difficult to keep track of.

Ham perspired freely. The goal of the cars became evident. They pulled up beside the tracks of a railroad which ran between Washington and New York. The men left the machines and scattered along the right of way, which was bordered by brush at this point.

Ham decided they were doing something with the railroad signal system. He kept a sharp lookout to make sure they did not tear up rails, or place anything on the tracks which might cause a wreck.

Since this district was frequently traversed by planes and one more was not likely to attract attention, Ham sank his ship a bit lower. If these men intended to endanger lives, he would interfere. Otherwise, he intended to play the role of observer. He was not optimist enough to believe that, single-handed, he could capture the crowd.

A rather long wait followed.

A TRAIN appeared, coming from the direction of Washington. It was one of the new streamlined trains. It must have been making around eighty miles an hour. Rounding a curve, it streaked down the straight stretch where the men Ham was observing had stationed themselves. Things began happening.

First, the block signal located ahead of the train changed, directing a stop. Then men popped up alongside the tracks, waving red flags.

Since there was no reason why he should do anything else, the engineer of the train applied the air. The streamlined cars came to a stop. The engineer alighted, evidently to ascertain what was wrong. Men leaped out of the brush beside the right of way and ran toward him. They held guns. The engineer put his hands up. More men ran down the side of the train and entered the coaches.

The whole thing was executed with great speed. The raiding party was inside the train scarcely more than two or three minutes. When they reappeared, they were escorting a prisoner. This individual was larger than any of his captors, and he kept his hands rigidly above his head. He was rushed to the waiting automobiles, which promptly sped away.

Ham happened to know that this particular railroad equipped its streamlined trains with a so-called wired-wireless system of communication, whereby the moving train could keep in touch with intermediate stations; but this must have been put out of commission by the raiders. A group of uniformed train officials left the stalled cars and dashed madly toward a distant farmhouse, evidently headed for a telephone.

Ham did not see more, his attention being centered on following the two cars. They were heading directly for the spot where the exchange from the other cars had been made. In fact, it developed when they reached that spot, the men intended to change back to their previous conveyances. They did so and resumed their journey.

The gyro was equipped with radio transmitting-and-receiving apparatus. The receiver was of the universal type in its wave band coverage. Ham turned it on and tuned it to police broadcasting wave lengths, and before long was rewarded with interesting information.

"Calling All New Jersey State Police!" intoned an official voice from the loudspeaker. *"Watch for two large black sedans, license numbers unsecured, occupied by gang of men estimated to exceed a dozen in number. Men held up Washington-to-New York railway train and took off Samuel Gerard Crowell, private secretary to Senator Lorton, chairman of the committee on tariff revision."*

There was more of it, having to do with the routine of the search for the two cars. This was not especially important, since the two machines had already been abandoned.

HAM did some concentrated thinking, which got him nowhere. He could not understand of just what value would such a prisoner as Crowell be?

Observing that the cars had turned into a roadside establishment, Ham put other thoughts from his mind. He throttled the gyro engine down so that it barely maintained his altitude, and made as little noise as possible. Then he rubbed his aching eyes and once more used the strong binoculars.

The place below seemed to be a summer camp and consisted of a large main building and a number of smaller bungalows, all situated on the shores of a small lake. At least one detail of the layout was interesting. There was a building on the lake shore built over the water, and it was too large for a mere boathouse. Ham hazarded a guess that it housed a seaplane.

The dapper lawyer continued his observation until he was certain the cars had reached their destination. He saw the machines put into garages. Shutting off the gyro motor, he headed the craft downward to the west of the camp where the blinding effects of the late afternoon sun would help prevent the aircraft being observed. He landed on the level floor of a dry creek, the only spot available in the wooded vicinity.

He got out and ran toward the camp, trailed rather closely by Chemistry and Habeas Corpus.

A MAN loafed on the rustic porch of the camp's largest building. A shotgun lay across his knees. A close observer might have noticed that he kept a sharp lookout over the vicinity. Another man was doing the same thing on the rear porch, and he also had a shotgun. Between them, they kept the surroundings under close observation.

Noise suddenly broke out in the brush some distance from the house. It was a not inconsiderable uproar, marked by squealings and squeakings. In fact, considering the kind of a noise it was and the locale, it was a startling sound. In a jungle infested by wild pigs and monkeys it might have been explainable, but here in the Jersey hills it was hard to account for.

"Bill!" yelled the fellow on the back porch. "What the hell's going on around there?"

"It's in the brush!" Bill explained. "Danged if I know what it is!"

So unique and so loud was this noise which had suddenly shattered the solitude of Jersey, that the two men joined each other in the yard and stood staring at the brush.

"Must be a couple of wampus cats," one grinned.

"They got them in Jersey?" the other asked, with entire seriousness.

His companion snorted.

"Come on," he said. "Let's look into this!"

The two men, with their shotguns ready, advanced into the brush. The undergrowth being thick, they had to make a little noise themselves.

The uproar ahead abruptly ceased, and there was a sound

as if two animals of not very impressive size were leaving the vicinity in great haste.

The two men ran forward, craning necks to see what they could. One fell down and got up, cursing. They were no woodsmen, and they did not care for the brush tearing their clothing. They stopped and jumped up and down like dogs looking for rabbits in a meadow. They did not, however, catch sight of the causes of the noise.

"Oh, well!" One shrugged. "Every little bit of excitement around this dead hole helps."

They trudged back to the house and took up their positions on the front and rear porches, shotguns ready across their knees. Having been gone only a few moments, and returning to find no visible change in the place, they took it for granted that everything was all right.

EVERYTHING was not all right—not from the standpoint of the two lookouts. They did not know that Ham had managed to get the two strange pets, Habeas and Chemistry, to stage a fight. Not that this took a great deal of ability, however. Habeas and Chemistry were ready to stage a fight almost any time. Under cover of the uproar which had drawn the two lookouts away, Ham had flitted across the clearing and was now inside the large building.

Ham had crawled through what looked like a basement window, and had found, much to his disgust, that there was no basement. The house rested on a foundation, about a yard off the ground, and the rock wall of this foundation was perforated with windows.

Ham was disgusted. He had run himself into a hole from which escape would be difficult. He crouched there, mentally chewing his finger nails, until his eyes, which had been used to the afternoon sunlight, accommodated themselves to the gloom underneath the house. It was then that Ham perceived that things were not as bad as they had at first seemed.

Almost over his head—he was well under the house—there was a trapdoor. The explanation for this completely defied him for a moment. Then he decided on the reason.

The trapdoor had been newly made. Somebody must have provided it for an escape!

Ham glanced about, then worked toward the rear. Because there seemed to be no harm in doing so, he struck matches. They afforded some light for his study of floor beams above his head, which were festooned with cobwebs. These cobwebs were scraped loose in some places. Ham found an area which was almost free of the sheer silky threads. Directly beneath this spot, he thumped the ground gently with a fist.

As he expected, there was a hollow sound. He scraped quietly with his hands and uncovered a square board. He lifted this and exposed the mouth of a shaft which was timbered.

Ham crawled back to the trapdoor, put an ear to it and caught a voice murmur; but the speakers did not seem to be in the room above. Ham put force against the trapdoor. It lifted hard. A moment later, he knew it came up under a settee or some other large article of furniture, and was covered by a rug.

The voices were quite distinct now, the words understandable.

SEVERAL men were talking and they seemed to be discussing another man, who was in difficulties.

"He'll be comin' out of it shortly," one said.

"He oughta!" growled another. "If you was careful with that chloroform."

"What was that noise outside?"

Some one must have gone out and questioned the two guards, because there was a noise of steps leaving, an interval, then they returned.

"Two rabbits or somethin' got to fightin' in the brush."

"Rabbits don't fight!"

"Well, it was somethin'. Didn't amount to nothin'. Look! Our friend, the senator's secretary, is comin' 'round."

That identified for Ham the man they had chloroformed. It was the fellow they had taken from the train. They must have drugged him to keep him quiet.

Ham listened intently. He heard an assortment of groans, such as might have come from a man in the act of regaining consciousness. There was a series of loud pops, as of hands on flesh. Evidently the victim was being slapped awake.

"Everything set?" demanded one of the captors, anxiously. "The adjustments should be made before he regains—"

"Shut up that fool talk!" another told him. "This guy isn't to know what the whole thing is about!"

A shrill voice began to sputter.

"What—what—what is the significance of this outrage?" it demanded.

That, Ham decided, was exactly the kind of voice that senators' secretaries should have—the voice of a young man who had too much dignity for his age.

"You know very well why you are here!" one of his captors growled.

"Why—why—I can't imagine!" snapped the senator's secretary. "I never saw you men before! Let me go! I've no money to pay you a ransom!"

"We don't want money!"

"Then what do you want?"

"Revenge!"

THERE was a short interval while the young man who was a prisoner tried to decide what they meant.

"Revenge?" he gulped. "I don't understand!"

A moment of silence followed. Ham, in his mind's eye, could see the men who were doing the questioning glaring at the captive.

"You lyin' little whelp! You *do* know what we're talkin' about!"

"I don't!" the prisoner exploded, hastily.

"It happened within the last ten days," he was told.

"But I don't recall anything." insisted the prisoner.

"Think hard." growled the other. "You'll recall it, all right. Maybe it didn't mean nothin' to you. But it sure meant a lot to a pal of ours. We're gettin' even for him, see?"

Ham, following the proceedings with all his attention, envisioned the prisoner thinking over every move he had made during the recent past. Ham also did some thinking himself. He had concluded these men were putting on an act, for they were not very good actors and their amateurishness had given them away.

What was their motive? Ham's best brow wrinkling failed to bring to mind anything that would explain the proceedings.

Apparently, the problem was too much for the prisoner, too.

"Please!" he exploded. "I've thought over every move I've made in the last two weeks. I can't think of a thing."

A man with a harsh voice asked, "What about it?"

Apparently, this question was not addressed to the senator's secretary.

"I'll see," said one of the men, in reply to the question.

Some one left the room where the interrogating was taking place. Three or four minutes elapsed. Then the one who had departed came back.

"It's all hunky dory," said the man who had left the room.

"What's the meaning of this insanity?" yelled the prisoner.

The man with the harsh voice laughed heartily.

"Buddy, I'm gonna have to beg your pardon," he said. "We've made what you might call a terrible big mistake."

"You mean I'm the wrong man?"

"You said it, buddy."

"I'll have you all in jail for this!" shrilled the prisoner, suddenly regaining his courage.

"Um-m-m!" muttered the harsh voice. "In that case, maybe we just better tie a rock to you and drop you in the lake, instead of turnin' you loose!"

There was a moment of horrified silence.

"No! No!" exploded the prisoner. "I won't tell any one about this!"

"Blindfold him," directed the leader. "Take him out."

The prisoner was not long on courage. He began to scream at the top of his voice, stopping only when a hand was evidently slapped over his mouth.

"Gag him!" directed the leader. "Take him away."

The young man was dragged out.

Chapter XIV

THE MAN WHO VANISHED

HAM had confidence in the cold-blooded villainy of the men above him, and was half convinced that he had just heard a murder ordered. He must stop that! He shoved against the trapdoor and a piece of furniture—it was a settee—slid away, making little noise, thanks to the muffling effects of a rug.

Ham tilted the trapdoor lid back and, in almost complete

silence, climbed up into a room. He was no sooner there than he wished he had not been so hasty, because he immediately heard words from the next room which assured him that murder was not to be done.

"You ain't gonna croak the kid?" one of the gang asked, anxiously.

"Nah!" said the man with the harsh voice. "Blindfold and gag him, take him over on the other side of the State somewhere, and dump him."

"That's the best out," agreed the other. "If he was to get killed, it'd stir up a fuss."

At that point, a man entered the next room in some haste. He was evidently carrying papers in his hands. Ham could hear them rustle.

"Well?" growled the coarse voice. "Did you get it all down in shorthand?"

"Most of it! Enough to make plenty of jack!"

"How does it read?"

"The tariff committee is gonna recommend that the import duty on Cuban sugar be reduced exactly fifty per cent," the man with the papers explained. "And what the committee recommends is pretty sure to get by the House, the Senate, and the president. That means the tariff will be reduced."

The coarse voice laughed. "That's swell! I'll get in touch with the big chief right away and we'll have brokers buying up the available supply of Cuban sugar in no time at all."

"How much do you think this will make us?"

"How the hell would I know?"

"I hope it's more than the Jethro Mandebran haul."

"It may be," said the other. "Anyway, this is more legitimate. We ain't comin' right out and stealin' the money. If they did catch us, I doubt if they could do anything."

"What about takin' that senator's secretary off the train? Ain't that kidnapin'?"

"Not for a smart lawyer. We didn't ask for ransom, did we?"

The man laughed heartily at his own explanation of just how simple the circumstances were.

Ham was hearing interesting things, and wanted to go on hearing them. He decided accordingly it might be a good idea to get back under the floor, and made a move to do this. But there is such a thing as being too cautious, especially when under a nervous strain.

The trapdoor slipped out of Ham's clutch and upset. Had the roof of the house fallen in, it could not have made a more disastrous noise.

Following the clatter, there was dead silence. Then some one cursed. Feet rattled on the floor, as men made a rush for the door.

Ham was a cautious soul. He was wearing one of Doc Savage's bulletproof chain mail undergarments, but that did not mean he cared to have the men shooting at him.

Diving a hand at his armpit, Ham produced from a padded holster one of Doc Savage's supermachine pistols. He pointed it at the door, and the thing let out an earsplitting moan as it dropped the so-called "mercy bullets" through the aperture.

The noise of the gun was so profoundly impressive that the charge of the men was halted.

There must have been a rack of high-powered rifles in the next room. The men used them to drive bullets through the walls. Laths and plaster of the partition offered little resistance.

HAM's legal training and practice had equipped him with an agile set of wits. He could think quickly at all times, but he was possibly at his best in a crisis, and proceeded to prove this now.

He seized the trapdoor, jammed it back in place, covered it with the rug and replaced the settee. The shooting, the thudding of rifle bullets, the clatter of falling plaster, the howling of the men, covered any noises he might have made.

Ham next raced to the window. It was closed. He opened it and unhooked the screen. This was to give the impression that he had come in by that route. The two guards who had been outside might wonder how he had managed to do this unobserved. However, that was their problem.

Working swiftly, Ham upset a chair near the window. It was his hope that the enemy would think this was what had made the clatter.

Ham now drew a deep breath. Bullets were smacking through the walls here and there. It was only by good fortune that he had not been hit, although a head wound would be the only kind which could disable him seriously, thanks to his bulletproof undergarment.

Ham eyed the opposite wall, then took a short run, jumped in the air and hit the wall feet first.

It was a partition giving into another room—not the room from which they were shooting. The building had been constructed for summer occupancy, and the partitions inside were of a composition board. This cardboardlike stuff surrendered. Ham went through to his waist, struggled violently, and then managed to negotiate the rest of the passage.

There was a tiny hallway, and a flight of rustic stairs. Ham raced up the stairs, found a door at the top and shoved through.

"You!" exploded a voice that might have belonged to a small boy. "Talk of the devil, and—"

Ham looked at Monk, who was tied up in ropes about as securely as a man could be.

"Who'd you think it was?" Ham demanded, producing a knife and starting on the ropes.

"An army, from the amount of shooting! Be careful with that dang knife! Where's my pet hog?"

"Around somewhere with Chemistry."

"He's in bad company," Monk growled. "Turn that other guy loose."

"What other guy?"

Monk pointed. "Where's your eyes?"

The upstairs section of the building was little more than an attic, and since there were no windows, it was comparatively dark in the recesses. Ham peered and discovered a figure he had missed before.

The individual was stout, gray-haired, with a pair of cheeks as ruddy as apples. Under ordinary conditions, he would have been a dignified gentleman with an air about him; but there is something about being tied hand and foot which dispels dignity.

Ham leaped over and began using the knife on the elderly gentleman's bindings. The latter was not gagged, and he spoke.

"What do you think our chances are of getting out of here alive?" he asked, calmly enough.

"Excellent!" said Ham. Always an optimist.

The elderly gentleman got to his feet. Some of his dignity automatically returned. Ham, who was one of the greatest living experts on sartorial matters, observed that the gentleman's suit was of expensive cloth and fine tailoring.

"Who," Ham demanded, "are you?"

"Jethro Mandebran," said the elderly man.

IT was not entirely necessary for Jethro Mandebran to reveal his name. Ham had already guessed his identity, having recognized the missing banker from pictures which had been printed by the newspapers. Ham peered about in search of other prisoners. The rest of the attic seemed devoid of inhabitants.

The gang downstairs was still shooting through the walls. No bullets had as yet sought out the upper portion of the house, so they probably thought Ham was still below.

The coarse-voiced man was shouting, and his orders had an ominous trend. He was directing some of his men to get outside and take up positions where they could cover the house and prevent any one from escaping.

"Where is your son, Alex?" Ham demanded of Jethro Mandebran.

A startling change came over the banker. His fists clenched, and his cheeks distinctly lost some of their ripe apple color.

"My son!" he yelled hoarsely. "Have they got him?"

The yell was heard below. A rifle bullet came up through the floor with an unpleasant rap, and missed Monk not more than six inches. The homely chemist bounced hastily to one side.

"If you got any rabbits in your hat," he told Ham, "you better pull 'em out. We're in a jam!"

"Just keep your hairy hide on!" Ham advised.

The dapper lawyer inserted a hand into a pocket and brought out a flat metal case which held two ammunition clips for his machine pistol. These bullets, however, were not charged with the chemical concoction which produced unconsciousness. What they held was of more violent nature.

Ham inserted one of the new drums in his machine pistol, ran to the stairs, leaned over and fired. He gave the trigger the briefest of pressures, to release not more than a dozen shots.

The result was annihilating. The rooms below filled with noise, splinters and reddish flame. It was as if lightning had struck a dozen times in one spot.

With a hasty gesture. Ham latched the machine pistol into single-shot position, the high explosive missiles being too precious to waste. Before launching more of them, he listened.

As was not unreasonable to expect, the men downstairs were suddenly giving all of their attention to getting out of the house. They had suffered damage. One fellow was screaming that he had a broken leg and demanding help, even threatening to shoot some one if he was not aided.

Ham released two more explosive bullets. They shook the house and hurried the exodus.

"Come on!" Ham ordered Monk and Mandebran. "If we give them time to get organized, we'll be out of luck!"

"My son!" gulped Jethro Mandebran.

"Monk!" Ham rapped. "Where'd they take young Alex Mandebran?"

"Somewhere else," Monk explained. "They said something about their boss wanting to question him."

"Come on!" Ham repeated.

The stairway was a wreck. Ham bounded hopefully to the lower floor, led the way into the adjacent room and, with wild haste, moved the settee and the rug and levered up the trapdoor.

They all dropped through, and Ham exposed the mouth of the tunnel shaft he had discovered previously.

"Hah!" Monk grunted. "I might have known he'd have a hole located!"

HAM took the lead, holstering his machine pistol so that dirt would not get in its mechanism when he started crawling. At the best, there is something ominous about crawling through a tunnel barely large enough to accommodate one's person. There were times when the bulky Monk, bringing up the rear, groaned that he would never make it. Thoughts of what would happen if the walls collapsed, pestered them.

Ham, controlling an overpowering desire to crawl as fast as possible, soon splashed into water and experienced a hideous feeling that the thing was flooded. This proved not to be the case, for it was only a puddle of seepage.

After he had crawled so far that it seemed certain they had traversed a large slice of the State of New Jersey, Ham bumped a wooden door. Fumbling, he found a latch, which he manipulated cautiously.

He was not surprised to find himself peering out into a large building which held an amphibian plane. The plane was not especially large; it was a single-motored cabin job. The ship had a new look, as if it had just come from a production line.

"This is a break!" Ham scrambled out of the tunnel. "Come on, you two!"

He ran for the ship. Monk and Jethro Mandebran hurried after him, looking vastly relieved. It was beginning to seem that they would make a get-away after all.

"This," declared Monk, "is gonna be a cinch!"

Monk had scarcely released the words, when the door of the plane popped open and revealed a man seated on the cabin floor. He held an automatic rifle. At that range, he could scarcely miss them.

"It's a cinch!" the man said. "If you don't think so, just make a funny move!"

Ham, Monk and Jethro Mandebran came to a dead stop, and seemed unable to think of anything to say.

The man with the automatic rifle remarked casually, "These bullets are copro-nickel and will go through that armor cloth stuff of Doc Savage's. We tried it, to make sure."

"How'd they find out about the chain mail undergarments?" Ham asked out of the side of his mouth.

"They took mine away from me after they grabbed me," Monk growled back at him. "Johnny was wearing one, too."

Jethro Mandebran breathed desperately, "Shall we make a break for it?"

If Ham and Monk were toying with that idea, they dismissed it when a man stood up from behind a gasoline drum in a corner, two automatic pistols in his hands. More men came in.

"We thought of watchin' this end of the tunnel first thing!" one of the newcomers grinned.

Ham was relieved of his machine pistol. A stout cord was employed to lash his wrists behind his back. Monk and Jethro Mandebran received the same treatment.

"We gotta find out what's to be done with you," one of the men said, and walked out.

HAM eyed Jethro Mandebran.

"What have they been doing with you?" he asked.

"That mystifies me," said Mandebran. "Nothing!"

"Nothing?"

"They just held me! They asked me questions about bank affairs and so on. I did not even answer the questions. Strangely enough, they did not insist on replies, nor did they torture me."

Ham asked dryly, "How about the twenty million that disappeared?"

"What?" Jethro Mandebran's eyes flew very wide.

"That sum has vanished from the bank which you control," Ham informed him.

"Why—why—" Jethro Mandebran choked. He was a picture of a profoundly startled and horrified elderly gentleman.

"Why," he exploded finally, "there was that much money available, but no one could have gotten their hands on it without knowledge which I alone possess!"

"That is what the authorities think," Ham remarked.

Jethro Mandebran became rigid. "You mean I am accused?"

"The police are doing a lot of wondering," Ham admitted.

At this point, four men marched in, picked up Jethro Mandebran and carried him out bodily.

Monk and Ham exchanged curious glances. Some five minutes later, the same four men walked in again.

"What'd you do with Mandebran?" Monk demanded, apprehensively.

The men did not reply. Their manner, however, as they laid hold of Monk and Ham, was ominous.

Ham did not like the look of it, and a horrible thought struck him. These fellows seemed not to be at all afraid, and it was incredible that they should be unafraid of Doc Savage. Could it be that the gang had managed to trap Doc? Had they disposed of him?

Chapter XV

THE GNARLED MAN

Doc Savage had not been disposed of, but he was having his difficulties. Incarcerated with Johnny and Sylvan Niles in the deep basement room of the old country house, escape from which was denied them by the steel plate which had closed the top of the dumb-waiter-like shaft, they were trapped. How thoroughly, they were not sure as yet.

Since the plate across the shaft was extremely solid, they were trying to dig up alongside it. For digging tools, they had demolished the bench and were using the big bolts which had held it together. Johnny, finishing his spell at the work, dropped down out of the hole. They were taking turns.

Doc Savage climbed up. He had taken the rubber heels from his shoes, split them into sheets with his pocket knife and had bound these around the longest bolt handle with a shirt sleeve. This insulating of the bolt was merely a precaution.

Johnny, having caught his breath somewhat, began throwing questions at Sylvan Niles. Johnny had occupied all his rest intervals in that fashion, but his success at uncovering anything new had not been a marked success.

"How do you and Hando Lancaster hook into this?" Johnny demanded.

"We don't," said the girl. "We were dragged in."

"How?"

"Through the spying and crookedness of a friend, so-called," retorted the young woman.

"Meaning young Alex Mandebran?"

"Meaning whoever you want to think?" she snapped.

"Be specific," Johnny requested.

"It must be a swell day outside, don't you suppose?"

"A predicational abnegation!" grumbled Johnny. He knew the girl would now start giving him snappy answers which meant nothing.

Unexpectedly, Doc Savage dropped down out of the hole which they were digging upward. The point of the bolt looked as if it had been placed for a time in the flame of a welding torch. Bluish smoke rolled down out of the hole.

"Electricity?" Johnny demanded.

The bronze man nodded.

"High amperage stuff carried by a network of insulated wires."

BONY Johnny peered doubtfully at the hole. He fumbled with an absent movement at the spot on the left side of his chest where his magnifying monocle usually dangled. This gesture meant that he was concerned.

"The wires can be cut?" he said, hopefully.

"Not with the equipment we have available," Doc Savage corrected. "The handle of this bolt is wrapped with all the insulating materials we have. It is not enough. Touching the wires gave me quite a shock through the handle."

Gaunt Johnny frowned. "Does that mean we are stuck?"

"Not exactly," Doc told him. "But it does mean we will have to try something that may conceivably result in our being buried alive."

"What is it?"

Doc Savage looked at the young woman. "Do you want to take a chance?"

"I might as well," she retorted. "If we're here when those men return, we might as well commit hara-kiri."

Without further explanation, the bronze man went to work. He drew from a pocket one of the tiny grenades which had wrought such havoc upstairs earlier. He opened this, doing it carefully by a process of unscrewing.

Doc completed dissection of the grenade without disastrous consequences. The explosive, once he had it in the palm of his hand, looked something like grease. He crawled up into the shaft and worked the stuff into the cracks at the edge of the metal plate. After some difficulty, he also wedged the detonator device of the bomb alongside the explosive.

"Get back!" he warned.

An instant later, he had set the timing device in operation, dropped down the shaft, leaped to the opposite side of the chamber, protecting head and face as well as he could with his arms. Johnny and Sylvan Niles did likewise.

Came a crash as if planets had collided. They distinctly felt the shock all over their bodies—sudden, violent pressure which left a feeling of tingling strangeness. Earth and débris tumbled down. Doc came erect and raced to the shaft mouth.

"I'll be superamalgamated!" gulped Johnny, also reaching the shaft.

The vertical tunnel seemed to have collapsed. The lower part of it was completely blocked.

THEY began to dig furiously. Dust choked them. They had to back away from the shaft and stand on tiptoe to breathe air that was comparatively free of dust. Johnny was perspiring freely. The girl was pale, grim. The explosive had thrown off fumes that nauseated them and stung their eyes.

They started digging again, and soon discovered the blast had shattered the steel barrier topping the shaft.

When finally they crawled out into the basement, it was dark. They breathed deeply, coughing and hacking to get rid of the dust, and slapped earth off their clothing.

"If you know a big word meaning hurrah, you might use it!" Sylvan Niles told scholastic Johnny in the darkness.

"When we get out in daylight, if it's still daytime, I'll do my best," Johnny replied.

"Maybe this'll help!" suggested a howling voice.

The electric lights came on. The light bulbs were of a 32-volt size, using current supplied by a small farm-type plant, and the lighting was not especially bright.

The light was enough, however, to disclose Hando Lancaster.

HANDO LANCASTER, at his best, was not a gentleman pleasant to look at. His round body, his tremendous head, his pipe-stem arms and legs, were unnatural. Too, his perpetual expression was that of a man who has just tried to consume a green persimmon.

Just now, his appearance was made more forbidding by the efficient-looking blue revolver which he held.

"Hando!" the girl gasped. "How did you find this place?"

Hando Lancaster's features twitched "I had a prisoner!" he screeched at the girl.

She nodded. "Yes! The one Doc Savage overpowered at the old brick factory. You carried him away when Doc was chasing the fellow's companions."

"I learned of this place from that prisoner," yelled Hando Lancaster. "It took me time! I got here and was searching, when I heard that explosion. I simply waited to see who was digging out."

Doc Savage changed his position slightly, and Hando Lancaster jutted his revolver in the bronze man's direction. "You stand still!"

Doc Savage studied the strange-looking fellow with the howling voice. "You are taking the wrong course, Lancaster."

"I've spent my life working on something that can change the whole course of human existence!" Hando Lancaster bellowed. "It's been stolen from me! The whelps who got it are using it to steal money!"

"Will you accept my aid in recovering your invention—as you call it?" Doc asked.

"No!"

"That makes it look as if you contemplate some crookedness of your own. Perhaps these other men just beat you to it."

Hando Lancaster squawled, "For thirty cents I'd shoot you!"

He looked as if he meant it.

Sylvan Niles interrupted hastily, attempting to calm the storm.

"Hando and I have spent every cent we possess on experiments," the girl explained. "Hando's idea is worth a fortune. It will do civilization an untold amount of good!"

"It is the greatest invention in history!" yelled Hando Lancaster.

"Exactly!" said the girl. "And we are darn well going to get paid for it. Call us greedy, if you want to."

Johnny was watching Doc Savage's metallic hands. The bronze man's fingers had been moving idly, as if he were nervous. This, however, was not the case. He was forming words in the deaf-and-dumb sign language, in the manipulation of which he and all of his aids were skilled.

"You're two crooks!" yelled Johnny, doing as Doc Savage had directed him by sign language.

Hando Lancaster stared to shift his gun toward Johnny. Doc Savage, displaying blinding speed, leaped and grabbed Hando Lancaster's gun.

Chapter XVI

THE BRONZE MAN MOVES

FIVE minutes later, the entire party—Doc Savage, Johnny, Sylvan Niles and Hando Lancaster—were in Hando Lancaster's car, a large sedan which looked shabby, but which seemed sound enough mechanically. The car had a large trunk on a rear rack.

Doc Savage was driving. Sylvan Niles rode beside him. In the rear seat, Johnny administered rather roughly to Hando Lancaster, who was just recovering from a clip on the jaw which Doc Savage had found necessary to give him.

Hando Lancaster opened his eyes, blinked several times, and put a fierce grimace on his large face. This came so near to being his usual expression that, strangely enough, he did not seem especially angry.

"An antipugnacious attitude is of inestimable signification," said Johnny.

Hando Lancaster frowned and gave several additional blinks.

"They didn't have words like that when I went to school!" he growled.

"If you're smart, you won't get tough," said Johnny, putting his earlier remark in simpler phraseology.

Hando Lancaster snorted, but he evidently thought it was good advice. He behaved.

Doc Savage was driving, and tooled the car along expertly at a high rate of speed. When they reached a village, Doc stopped the car, left Johnny to watch the other two, entered a newsstand and bought a late edition of a paper. He walked out of the drugstore reading the newspaper, and on reaching the car, handed it to Johnny.

"Take a look at that!" he suggested.

Johnny knew the bronze man was referring to the headlines:

GANG HALTS FAST TRAIN
SENATOR'S SECRETARY TAKEN

Hando Lancaster leaned forward and stared steadily for several moments, reading the headlines and a part of the story below. The story explained the senator was head of the sugar tariff revision committee.

"Want to tell us what that means?" Doc Savage asked him.

Hando Lancaster only stared.

"I'll tell you," the girl spoke up, unexpectedly. "It's worth it, if we can keep that gang from—"

"Shut up!" yelled Hando Lancaster.

"Use your head!" the girl snapped at him. "Those men stand a chance to make millions—"

"They're not robbing anybody, are they?" retorted Hando Lancaster.

"Yes, they are!" asserted the girl. "That senator's secretary probably knows what is to be done about the sugar tariff. These men will jump in and buy or sell sugar, and will take profits that should go to the people who grow and handle the sugar."

"Shut up!" yelled Hando Lancaster

Without saying a word, Doc Savage got behind the wheel and drove on. He headed for New York City. If the girl and Hando Lancaster expected him to question them, they got a surprise, for he addressed no inquiry whatever to them.

Doc drove directly to the skyscraper which housed his headquarters. He did not put Hando Lancaster's sedan in the basement garage, but parked it in a side street near the skyscraper.

Without persuasion, Hando Lancaster and the girl accompanied Doc Savage and Johnny into the building. It was significant that Lancaster and the girl, both virtual prisoners, did not call on a policeman for help, although they passed within a few feet of one and the officer saluted Doc smartly.

They took Doc's private elevator to the eighty-sixth floor, stepped out into the severely plain modernistic corridor and approached the metal door entering into Doc's headquarters.

"Wait here," Doc Savage directed.

Leaving the others behind, Doc entered the reception room. There he did a thing which would have surprised Johnny, had he seen it. Doc got an ordinary-looking revolver from a case. He carried this through the library, selected a large, overstuffed chair and thrust the gun down beside the cushion. It was out of sight there, but any one sitting in the chair would be almost certain to feel its hard bulk.

Doc went back and admitted the others.

"There might have been enemies hidden here," he explained.

Doc guided Hando Lancaster and Sylvan Niles into the library, waved at chairs and requested, "Take seats."

Hando Lancaster occupied the chair which was most convenient to him when Doc Savage issued the invitation. This chanced to be the chair with the gun concealed beside its cushion.

Johnny left the room to change from the breechcloth he was still wearing, to some street clothes. He came back quickly.

Going to a telephone—there were extension telephones in all parts of the place—Doc Savage got a long distance operator.

"Get me Senator Lorton, in charge of the senatorial committee on tariff revision," the bronze man requested.

The wait was short enough to be a compliment to the efficiency of modern telephone communication. Doc Savage made his identity known to Senator Lorton. Evidently, the bronze man's name and reputation were familiar to the legislator, because there was no preliminary negotiating before Doc launched into the heart of the matter on his mind.

"Your secretary, Samuel Gerard Crowell, was seized this afternoon by a group of unscrupulous men who desire to know what the senatorial committee has decided to do about the sugar tariff question," the bronze man said. "Your secretary undoubtedly knew what the committee had decided to do."

"He did," admitted Senator Lorton. "But my secretary was asked no questions about the sugar tariff. I have just talked to him—his kidnapers released him, not long ago—and he stated explicitly he was not lying."

"Nevertheless, the information was probably secured from him," Doc Savage said. "Are you familiar enough with my name to take my word that the information was secured?"

The senator hesitated for a long time. "I'll assume you know what you are talking about."

"The men who got the information undoubtedly intend to use it to trade on the sugar market. If the tariff is raised, any domestic sugar they buy now can be sold for more money a bit later. Can you do something about that?"

"I certainly can!" said Senator Lorton. "I will explain to the committee that we must pigeonhole this bill for an indefinite period. Would that do the trick?"

"It would," Doc told him. "And thank you."

"I would like to have more details on this."

"You will get them," Doc assured him. "Later."

The conversation was terminated.

During the conversation, the bronze man had been watching the windows—but not because he was interested in the view. He could see Hando Lancaster's reflection in one of the windows.

Doc had seen Lancaster give a slight start, then casually insert a hand between the cushion and the side of the chair in which he sat. Hando Lancaster had discovered the presence of the gun.

"I'll be back in a few minutes!" Doc Savage said to Johnny.

The bony geologist was occupying a chair near the window. He had secured a machine pistol from the lockers in the laboratory where the weapons were kept. He was not holding this in his hands, but had placed it on a small table beside his chair. If he needed the weapon, he would have to reach for it.

Doc Savage left Johnny sitting there, watching the two prisoners, and walked into the laboratory. Once in there, Doc moved swiftly, leaping to the rear of the large room. Here he manipulated hidden locks, and caused a panel in the wall to open.

Doc stepped through the panel; it closed behind him. A magnifying glass would have been necessary to find a trace of the spot where he had disappeared.

IN the library, Johnny watched his two prisoners idly. Neither said a word, but both looked very ill at ease. Hando Lancaster seemed to be scratching his right thigh.

"Cerebration might be expedient," Johnny suggested.

"Eh?" said Hando Lancaster, who did not seem to be up on long words.

"Think it over!" Johnny translated. "If you've got good judgment, you'll decide to throw in with Doc Savage. Only crooks buck the big bronze fellow."

That last remark was scarcely tactful, and it caused Sylvan Niles to glare indignantly.

"I'm no crook!" she snapped. "You should realize that by now!"

"Your actions haven't indicated as much," Johnny reminded her.

"What does *this* indicate to you?" Hando Lancaster asked, suddenly.

Johnny looked, and became a rigid linkage of bones when he found himself scrutinizing the business end of a revolver. The presence of a gun in Hando Lancaster's hand smacked of black magic to Johnny, the gaunt geologist not having seen Hando bring it up from between and beside the cushion of the chair in which he sat.

"Unless you figure you're bulletproof, you'd better sit still," said Hando Lancaster. "And don't reach for that trick pistol there by your elbow."

Johnny was not exactly without caution, so he sat still. He did his best to peer into the revolver's chambers to see if the weapon was loaded, but the light was wrong.

"Sylvan, get his gun!" Hando Lancaster directed.

The young woman complied with the request.

Hando Lancaster heaved a sigh of relief when Johnny was disarmed. Then the spiderlike inventor left his chair, came forward and gouged Johnny's stomach with the revolver muzzle.

"We're taking you as a hostage!" said Hando Lancaster.

The girl objected, "But that will only get us into more trouble!"

"Pipe down!" suggested Hando Lancaster. "From now on, I'm going to use a different system! People are going to stop walking on me, if they know what's good for them."

"Nobody's been walking on you," Sylvan Niles told him, frostily.

"The heck they ain't!"

Johnny was urged toward the door. Hando Lancaster managed to do an excellent job of watching Johnny and the laboratory door at the same time. Hando evidently feared Doc Savage would appear. The bronze man did not.

Five minutes later, Johnny found himself seated in Hando Lancaster's ancient sedan. The car got into motion.

THE sedan had once been a sumptuous machine. Upholstery was of good quality, although worn and in need of cleaning. There was a clock mounted in the back of the front seat, so that those riding in the rear could tell time without craning their necks. This was an electric clock and it was running.

It rewound itself with a rather loud *click,* which called Johnny's attention to the time. Later, it wound itself again, and Johnny noted that the elapsed time was exactly half an hour. The clock was evidently old, or it would not rewind itself so often.

It turned out that the rewinding activities of the clock were to be Johnny's only method of judging the passage of time, for, once they were outside the confines of the city, the gaunt geologist was blindfolded and forced to lie on the car's floorboards. He listened to the engine, trying to judge how fast they were going. This was difficult, because it was an old and noisy engine and probaby sounded as if it were going a good deal faster thán it was.

Once, the car turned sharply and bumped for a short distance over what was evidently a rough side road. It came to a stop, the engine died, and they remained parked there for some time. The only piece of conversation was very short, and enlightened Johnny not at all.

"Hando," said Sylvan Niles, "I think we're doing the wrong thing."

"Leave it to me," retorted Hando Lancaster.

"Possibly we should have told Doc Savage the whole story," said the girl. "It's likely he will find out, anyway."

"Not if I can help it, he won't!"

After that, there was deep silence. The car engine seemed to have overheated a little, and Johnny could hear the radiator boil for a time. The sound finally subsided, but Johnny did not believe they had stopped because of the overheating of the engine. A remark made by Hando Lancaster finally told him the guess was correct.

"Nobody following us!" said Hando Lancaster. "I've watched the road, and there's not an airplane in sight. It's safe to go on."

"Where?" the girl asked him.

"I'll show you," said Hando Lancaster. "I fixed us up a neat place!"

The car backed out of the rough side road onto an asphalt highway. Johnny, even blindfolded, could tell the difference between asphalt and conćrete pavement. Concrete slabs have expansion joints at intervals, and cause a series of slight bumps as car wheels passed over them.

The clock reset itself twice before the car finally came to a stop.

Chapter XVII

THE MENTAL TELEPATHER

JOHNNY, still blindfolded, was hauled out of the car. Hando Lancaster seemed to have a great deal of strength, despite his gnarled stature.

Try as he would to look down his nose under the blindfold, Johnny had no luck. He endeavored to use his ears, but Hando Lancaster had left the noisy car engine running and its uproar blanketed all small sounds.

Johnny took several deep breaths through his nose. The girl evidently realized he was trying to catch some scent which would identify his surroundings, and promptly grabbed his nose and held it, forcing him to breathe through his mouth so that he could not smell effectively.

"I'll fix that!" said Hando Lancaster.

A moment later, a small quantity of gasoline was dumped on Johnny's face. The strong tang of the stuff overcame all other scents.

"It'd make it simpler if we knocked him out," growled Hando Lancaster.

He did not do this, however, but lifted Johnny and carried him. Johnny, who had expected to be transported only a short distance, was surprised when Hando Lancaster walked for some time. Finally there came a series of jars, and Johnny decided he was being carried down a long flight of stairs. He distinctly caught the odor of wet earth, of dampness. He was, he decided, being taken to a subterranean cavern somewhere.

Johnny, had his blindfold been removed, would have received quite a shock. He would also have been disgusted with his own perceptive abilities. Hando Lancaster had walked quite a distance, it was true, but his walking had been done in a small circle. Now, by a series of short jumps, he had succeeded in giving the impression to Johnny that they were descending steps, when, as a matter of fact, they were still on level ground.

The girl had picked up a handful of damp earth and was holding it where Johnny could get its scent through the gasoline fumes.

Though quite confident he was underground, Johnny heard himself being carried across a wooden floor and through a door. Metal came under the feet of the man who carried him. Then Johnny was dumped with a painful thump on a hard steel floor.

The blindfold was removed from his eyes. He blinked. Intense darkness was all about him.

Blinding light leaped from a flashlamp in Hando Lancaster's hand, and its roving luminance showed the steel wall of a cubicle scarcely more than eight feet square. The metal had once been red-leaded and painted, but the paint had scaled off, and there was a great deal of rust.

Both Sylvan Niles and Hando Lancaster were present.

Johnny now demanded indignantly, "What's the idea of this?"

"Glory be!" said Sylvan Niles. "You do use little words once in a while, don't you?"

"Keep him here," Hando Lancaster directed.

HANDO LANCASTER walked out of the steel cell of a room, his manner determined, as if he had something definite in mind. During the interval when he was gone—about five minutes— Johnny looked around with great interest, endeavoring to ascertain where he was. The steel chamber had no windows. The only opening was a door, and it was narrow. The place smelled of dampness and rust.

Hando Lancaster came back, walking gingerly. In his arms he carried an array of complicated-looking apparatus. He put this down near the door and began sorting it out. His touch was almost loving.

Johnny had been connected with Doc Savage long enough to recognize most ordinary types of scientific devices. He looked over Hando Lancaster's outfit and noted several battery boxes. There was also a pair of large cases covered with dials, and with little inspection ports, through which intricate-looking vacuum tubes could be seen. The thing, Johnny decided instantly, was something Hando Lancaster had created himself.

Stare as he would, Johnny gathered not the slightest idea of what the thing was.

Hando Lancaster attached two peculiar-looking headsets to the devices. These headsets were unusual in appearance. They were literally cages of wires and glass tubes.

One of the things was placed over Johnny's head. It was heavy.

"You break that and I'll knock your brains out!" said Hando Lancaster, seriously.

Johnny had been contemplating just that, but the man sounded so earnest that he changed his mind.

Hando Lancaster placed the other headgear carefully over his own cranium. He squatted beside the boxes and fiddled with the dials and switches. Johnny waited for something to happen. He half expected to be electrocuted, but as far as he could tell, nothing whatever occurred.

Hando Lancaster began to grin widely. He was a grotesque-looking bug of a chap under the headgear.

"Who do you think is the main villain behind all this mystery?" Hando Lancaster asked, abruptly.

Johnny had, of course, considered that question before and had concluded that Hando Lancaster himself looked as much like a mastermind as anybody. The girl, of course, was working with him, Johnny had concluded. Yet he was reluctant to think her thoroughly villainous. Rather, she must have been deceived by Hando Lancaster. Probably, the fellow had told her whatever he was doing was perfectly legitimate, and she had believed him.

"I haven't the slightest idea who is the brains," Johnny said.

"You're a liar!" Hando Lancaster told him. "You think I'm the mastermind."

Johnny blinked and his mouth came open.

"Furthermore, I have not deceived Sylvan Niles, as you think," Hando Lancaster snapped.

Johnny swallowed several times. To say that he was stunned, was putting it mildly. He was dumfounded. The man was reading his mind!

"Exactly!" said Hando Lancaster.

"Huh?" Johnny exploded.

"I am doing exactly what you think I am doing," Hando Lancaster told him. "Reading your mind."

WILLIAM HARPER LITTLEJOHN was an erudite soul, far more filled with learning than the average individual. He was so educated, in fact, that he seldom saw anything happen which he could not explain instantly. His life had been a hectic one, especially since he had joined up with Doc Savage. Yet, not often had he been completely baffled.

He was baffled now. Further, he was profoundly amazed. It was impossible, of course, that Hando Lancaster could be reading his mind. There must be a trick.

"I'll fool the guy," Johnny thought. By concentrating, he cast his memory back. He thought of an incident, months in the past, when he had gone through some hair-raising encounters with what had at first appeared to be monsters, but which had later turned out to be nothing but oversize lizards.

"What was I just thinking about?" Johnny demanded.

"You are testing me by thinking about some big lizards which you encountered some months ago," said Hando Lancaster.

Johnny would not have been more dazed by a blow on the head with a hammer. The man *was* reading his mind!

Hando Lancaster came over, removed his apparatus from Johnny's spinning head and carried it toward the door with infinite care, evidently planning to take it outside where it would be safe.

He was backing through the door, when a pair of sinewy bronze hands jumped from concealment beside the door and grasped Hando by the nape of the neck.

Hando Lancaster had self-control. He did not want to smash his apparatus, and he lowered it carefully to the floor before he started to fight.

He tried to reach a pocket, but Doc Savage trapped his arms, preventing that move. Doc tore the pocket from the suit, and a gun fell to the floor. Sylvan Niles ran for the weapon. Doc Savage got in her way, still holding his prisoner.

Shoving both Hando and the girl into a corner, Doc managed to keep them there, thwarting easily their lunging attempts at escape.

Johnny flounced around on the floor, trying without much success to loosen the bonds which held his wrists and ankles.

"I'll be superamalgamated!" he barked. "How'd you get here, Doc?"

"Hando's car," Doc explained, "has a large trunk."

Hando Lancaster squawled, "You were in that trunk?"

The bronze man nodded. It then dawned on Hando Lancaster that he had been tricked throughout.

"You planted that gun beside the chair cushion!" he screeched. "I'll bet it wasn't even loaded!"

"It wasn't!" Doc Savage admitted.

Sylvan Niles looked at Hando Lancaster accusingly.

"I told you he would get the best of us," she said. "We should have taken him into our confidence."

Hando Lancaster glowered at Doc Savage. "Why did you trick me into leading you here?"

Doc pointed at the contraption which had been used on Johnny.

"To get hold of one of those things," he said.

HANDO LANCASTER and Sylvan Niles, realizing that they were wasting time trying to escape, stopped resisting and sulked in the corner.

Doc untied Johnny, then used the ropes which had been on Johnny's ankles to secure Hando Lancaster's wrists and ankles.

Then the bronze man assured Sylvan Niles, "If you try to run, we shall have to tie you also."

"I'll stay!" she snapped.

Doc dragged Hando Lancaster to the center of the steel room, then brought the strange apparatus over. Doc spent several minutes examining the device, which seemed to pain Hando Lancaster so much that he groaned loudly.

"Your life's work, eh?" Doc asked.

Hando Lancaster only moaned.

"Judging from the care with which you were handling it, this must be the only one you have left?" Doc suggested.

The spiderlike man did not reply.

As a part of the preparations for his unusual career, Doc Savage had studied many subjects intensively. Electricity was one of the sciences in which he had majored, and few living men had a greater general knowledge of electricity.

Lifting the headgear, which had been on Johnny, he fitted it over Hando Lancaster's head.

"You want to do the receiving?" Doc asked Johnny.

"Will the thing really work?"

"Try it and draw your own conclusions."

Johnny hesitated. The device had seemingly accomplished

such a confoundingly impossible thing that he was skittish about trying it. Finally, he shrugged and permitted the other headset to be fitted over his brow. Doc then began adjusting knobs and switches.

"If my mishandling endangers the device, you might tell me," he requested of Hando Lancaster.

"Turn the filament control knobs of the current amplifier back about three points," Hando Lancaster growled. "They're in the upper right hand corner. I made those amplifier tubes myself, and I don't want them burned out. I haven't got replacements!"

"I don't think the thing will work!" Johnny interposed, emphatically.

"It operates on a perfectly sound principle," Doc Savage said, adjusting the knobs. "It is well known to scientists, and has been for some time, that tiny electrical currents are generated in the human brain. These currents are infinitesimal, only millionth parts of volts."

"Oh!" said Johnny. "I begin to catch on!"

"Many experimenters have succeeded in detecting the presence of the current by rigging supersensitive galvanometers around the heads of human subjects," Doc Savage told him. "A galvanometer is merely a device which indicates the presence of an electric current."

Johnny frowned and seemed to be trying to concentrate. "I don't hear anything," he said.

"And you won't," Doc Savage told him. "Just relax. Don't try to think of anything."

JOHNNY shut his eyes in an effort to do this. For several moments there was absolutely no sound.

"Do some thinking, so he can pick it up," Doc Savage told Hando Lancaster.

The latter only glared.

More moments of waiting ensued. Johnny began to wear an air of intense concentration. Finally, his jaw began to sag.

"I'll be superamalgamated!" he exploded.

"You are beginning to see how it works?" Doc Savage asked him.

"I certainly am!" Johnny replied. "I don't hear anything or see anything. A series of thoughts just pass through my mind! I know darn well they're not my thoughts, because I don't know anything about the subjects with which they are concerned!"

The bronze man nodded. "The device on Hando Lancaster's head is a supersensitive antenna," he said. "It picks up the electric field created by his thought waves. They are amplified and—through the transmitter antenna which you are wearing—implanted upon the nerves in the cells of your own brain."

"Simple!" said Johnny, dizzily.

"That is only the roughest kind of an explanation," Doc Savage assured him. "Actually, the process is highly involved, amazingly complicated. But that is substantially how it is done."

"An ultra-prodigiosity!" said Johnny.

"What is Hando Lancaster thinking?" Doc Savage asked.

JOHNNY sat silent for some time.

"He is thinking that he would like to wring both our necks," he said, and frowned reprovingly at Hando Lancaster.

Hando Lancaster returned an indignant glare, but said nothing. There was more silence.

"He is thinking about the years he spent developing this thought telepathy device," Johnny said. "He is thinking how he and his secretary, Sylvan Niles, spent all their money on their experiments. They went abroad to have a foreign scientist make up some of the highly complicated vacuum tubes which they needed."

"Excellent!" Doc Savage said.

Johnny continued, "Hando Lancaster is thinking of meeting young Alex Mandebran abroad. He is wondering how Alex Mandebran could have learned of the existence of the mental telepathy apparatus. He is also wondering how Alex Mandebran managed to steal his secret."

"I've done some wondering on that score myself," Sylvan Niles interjected.

"Please be still!" Johnny told her. "Hando Lancaster is now thinking what a fiendish devil Alex Mandebran is, to seize his own father and carry him away and subject him to examination with the mental telepathy device in order to learn how to rob his poor father's bank of all those securities."

Johnny began to look rather excited.

"Doc!" he exploded. "Hando Lancaster knows absolutely that Alex Mandebran is the brains behind this whole affair! Hando Lancaster got that information from the prisoner whom you captured for him out of the old factory building."

The girl stared at Hando Lancaster.

"Hando!" she gasped. "You did not tell me that you had absolute proof of Alex Mandebran's guilt."

There was a noise from the doorway, a significant noise. It drew all eyes.

Three men, all the narrow opening would accommodate, were wedged in the door. They had their hands full of guns.

"You people are finding out too blasted much!" one said, grimly.

Chapter XVIII

CLEANUP PLANS

IF Doc Savage moved a muscle, it was not noticeable; but Johnny was not as composed. He wrenched the complicated headgear off his brow, placed it on the floor and scrambled erect.

"You're kind of a thin target," one of the gunmen in the door told him. "But I believe I could hit you."

Johnny clenched his fists, but he used excellent judgment and stood still.

"You've got us in a fine spot!" Sylvan Niles snapped at Doc Savage.

The bronze man said nothing.

Entering the steel cubicle with extreme caution, two of the newcomers proceeded to search Doc Savage and Johnny for weapons. They seemed surprised to find none on the bronze man's person, although they removed his coat, patted his trouser legs, searched under his shirt, and even yanked off the bullet-proof chain mail undergarment which he always wore.

Several more men appeared. All were heavily armed.

"How did you get here?" Hando Lancaster screamed at them.

"Shut up!" one told him. "We've had men following you. You came here and looked this place over a week ago. One of our men was on your trail."

"Blast you!" shrieked Hando Lancaster.

"There'll be some blasting, if you don't pipe down!" he was informed.

A man came bearing a new, sound rope, and Doc Savage's wrists were lashed behind him.

One of the men nudged Hando Lancaster's mental telepathy apparatus contemptuously.

"This is one of the first models," he sneered. "The receiving antenna has gotta be on a guy's head before it'll work. Now, with the newer models of the set—"

"Which you stole from me!" Hando Lancaster screamed.

"With the newer models," the man continued, as if there had been no interruption, "reception of the thought waves is possible at a distance of eight to ten feet, under favorable circumstances. Of course, the closer the subject is to the antenna, the better."

Doc Savage and the others were herded out of the room. They were led down a narrow, rust-strewn corridor. There were boards underfoot, and they were rotten for the most part. The walls were rusty steel.

They mounted a flight of decrepit, ladderlike stairs, and Johnny suddenly realized where they must be.

"A ship!" he exploded.

"One of the abandoned War-time bulks, tied up in Chesapeake Bay," Doc Savage hazarded. "An excellent hideaway!"

On an upper deck, they were guided into what had once been a dining room for the crew, judging from the long benches and tables which were still in place.

On one of the tables stood a complicated mass of apparatus. It was only a little more bulky than Hando Lancaster's. One of the men pointed at it.

"That's the new model!" he said, and scowled at Doc Savage. "We're gonna use it on you. We've been planting the pick-up antenna in things like chairs and mummy cases."

THEY were evidently surprised at the fact that Doc Savage was offering no resistance. Johnny was also puzzled, but kept quiet about it. Doc did not usually permit himself to be hustled about in this manner.

The bronze man was forced to seat himself on a bench.

The antenna of the telepathic pick-up contrivance was not fitted on his head, but merely placed on the bench near him. A man donned the receiving antenna, which was a compact headset.

"Keep everybody else away from here," this operator warned.

Evidently this device, while it was more sensitive than the other, was subject to picking up interference from persons who might be standing near by.

The operator adjusted the knobs carefully, then leaned back and shut his eyes in an attitude of frowning concentration. It quite frequently requires concentration not to think. For three or four minutes, there was absolute silence.

"Damn the luck!" cursed the man doing the receiving.

"What is it?" some one asked him.

"The bronze man knows that the chief is Alex Mandebran!" grated the operator.

"Well, why get fussed up about that?" snorted the other. "We already suspected he knew, didn't we?"

"That ain't the worst of it!" barked the operator.

"What?"

"What time is it?"

One of the men consulted a watch. "Ten o'clock."

"Here's the dig," said the operator. "The bronze guy is thinking that he'll be rescued and all of us will be in the can at exactly midnight!"

This information was not received with what could be called glee.

"What's gonna happen?" a man said.

There was a wait, while the man with the receiving antenna tried to get additional information out of Doc Savage's brain.

"Whew!" he said. "This bird thinks like chain lightning!"

"How does he figure he's gonna get out of this jam?" snapped one of the group. "An' how does he figure we're gonna land in the can?"

There was another wait.

"No use!" snapped the operator. "He's stopped thinkin'!"

"Stopped?"

"Well, not exactly," the man muttered, uneasily. "He is thinking about how we will all probably draw life terms for grabbing old Jethro Mandebran and the twenty million."

"Better see what the chief wants to do about this," one suggested.

The man departed. Shortly, he was back.

"The chief says to put them with the other prisoners," he advised.

Doc Savage, Sylvan Niles, Hando Lancaster and Johnny were led down a companionway, along a corridor, and jammed into a large chamber which bore a resemblance to a stateroom. There was one porthole, too small for any one to climb through.

The four prisoners were jammed into the room. The door was slammed behind them.

"We gotta watchman on deck," one of the guards advised. "The first guy who sticks his head out of that porthole and starts yelling, is gonna stop a bullet!"

Doc Savage ran a glance over the three prisoners which the room already held.

Monk and Ham were there and looked the worse for wear. The third man, Jethro Mandebran—Doc recognized him easily from newspaper pictures—was managing to maintain his dignity, though bound hand and foot. His gray hair was tousled.

Monk gulped unbelievingly, "You're not a prisoner, Doc?"

The gaunt Johnny answered that one, using small words.

"I suppose you think these ropes are on us for ornaments?" he snapped.

Monk groaned noisily.

"Stop that, you hairy crape-hanger!" Ham said, peevishly.

"But we'll never get out of this," Monk complained. "These guys'll shoot us!"

"They've taken over my hiding place here!" Hando Lancaster bleated. "We'll never get help! No one ever visits this place!"

Elderly, dignified Jethro Mandebran broke into the dour recital with a cheerful note.

"We have seen no sign of my son, Alex," he said.

"So what?" Sylvan Niles snapped.

"Alex has probably escaped," Jethro Mandebran told her. "I am confident that he will manage to rescue us."

The young woman drew a deep, shaky breath. She seemed on the point of informing the rather pompous old man that his son was the mastermind responsible for their present straits. But she must not have had the heart. She remained silent.

Hando Lancaster, however, held no such qualms.

"Alex is behind all this!" he informed the old man, giving the information in a yell, his habitual manner of speech.

The statement was too big a lump for elderly Jethro Mandebran to comprehend all at once.

"What are you saying?" he asked, hoarsely.

"Your son, Alex!" Hando Lancaster howled. "He's the brains of this thing!"

Old Jethro Mandebran seemed to melt like a tallow candle to which a hot flame has been applied. He had been standing. Now, he sat down slowly.

"That isn't true," he moaned. "I won't believe it!"

"You wouldn't!" Hando Lancaster snapped. "But it's a fact!"

"Alex!" the old man gasped. "Alex—oh—oh—"

Chapter XIX

THE IMAGINATION FIGMENT

ELDERLY Jethro Mandebran's grief was a pitiful thing to see. The old man had iron in his make-up, for he had stood staunchly under the shadow of knowing that he would have to prove to the authorities, if he ever escaped his captors, that he had not absconded with the fabulous sum of money which was missing from his bank.

The story that he had been seized in order that a mind-reading device might be used on him by a gang of crooks, who had found out in this manner how to get the money and had taken it, was a thin story. Almost any policeman would laugh himself purple in the face after listening to it. Jethro Mandebran had known, undoubtedly, that he must make this story believable or go to prison. That knowledge had not shattered his self-control.

But the information that his son was the brains behind the affair, had wrecked him. He was a broken old fellow, lost in a swamp of grief. The world, for him, had become a cruel and horrible thing.

It was a long time before any one spoke. Even Hando Lancaster was silent, as if regretting what he had told the old man.

It was Monk who squeaked finally, his small voice more than usually shrill, "Have you got any kind of a plan, Doc?"

"We'll wait," Doc Savage told him.

Johnny eyed the bronze man.

"What did that stuff about our getting out of this at midnight mean?" the bony geologist asked. "The stuff their machine told them you were thinking about?"

Doc Savage did not answer.

"I'll confess I'm uneasy," Johnny continued.

"Do not talk about it!" Doc Savage directed.

"Huh?"

"Their telepathic pick-up antenna may be located close to us," Doc said. "If they can find out what the plan is, they can thwart it."

"Oh!" said Johnny. "I see!"

If Doc Savage was having difficulty keeping his thoughts confined to channels which would give their captors no information, he received material assistance some five minutes later when the door opened and a man came in. The fellow carried a large bundle of old burlap sacks. He went to the porthole.

The glass, as they had all noticed, was missing from the port. In fact, the whole rim of the porthole was gone, evidently having been salvaged in the past. Into this opening, the man began stuffing the burlap sacks. He kept at his task until he had the aperture thoroughly stoppered. Then he made a careful examination of the prisoners' bonds.

"I guess you won't do much moving around," he said.

The man now walked out; but he was back an instant later, carrying a cardboard box. The open top of this bulged with excelsior.

The man began picking the excelsior out. He was careful at his task, and when he straightened, he was holding a fat glass jug, which had been packed in the carton.

He held the jug in the glow of a flashlight, where Doc Savage could see.

"You able to guess what this stuff is?" the man asked.

Doc eyed the jug's contents. Liquid. The stuff had a characteristic color, too.

"Hydrocyanic acid," the bronze man hazarded.

"Check!" agreed Monk, who had not been asked to comment.

"If I dropped this, what would happen?" the man asked.

"You would probably die before you got to the door," Monk offered, hopefully. "That stuff makes a vapor, the effects of which are among the quickest and most deadly known."

"What I meant," the man leered, "is what would happen if I threw the stuff in from the door and then slammed the door?"

No one spoke.

"It's the boss's idea!" said the man.

At last, Jethro Mandebran gasped, "Alex—my son—ordered—"

He seemed to choke.

Then there was a shout in the corridor, the sound of running feet, and a man appeared. He wore a worried expression, and this cleared when he saw the prisoners were unharmed.

"What can we do about it besides croak the prisoners and clear out of here?" asked the man with the hydrocyanic acid.

"We're gonna use the telepathic apparatus on Doc Savage again," announced the other, "and see what we can get outta him. Bring him along!"

Doc Savage was seized. Four men carried him out, and back to the dining room. He was placed on the table near the receiving antenna of Hando Lancaster's remarkable invention.

A MAN donned the receiving headset, and fiddled with the controls until he had the adjustment right. It seemed to be a very delicate matter, this getting an adjustment.

"All right," the man said.

Instantly, another fellow dashed forward and delivered a terrific blow with a gun to Doc Savage's face. He struck again. The blows were calculated to produce great pain, rather than unconsciousness.

The man who had done the beating retreated hastily from the zone of the receiving antenna.

"That oughta make it hard for him to keep from thinkin' about whatever plan he's got," the fellow gritted.

There was an expectant silence.

"Got it!" yelled the man doing the receiving.

The others dashed forward.

"What is it?"

"The bronze guy knew where this place was, before he came here," exploded the operator. "He told the State police! Troopers have got us surrounded!"

More than one man swore fearfully at that information.

"Quiet!" ripped the man who had used the receiver. "There's a way outta this. If the bronze guy appears on the bridge and turns a flashlight on himself to show that he's all right, the troopers have orders to withdraw and let him handdle the thing to suit himself."

A man barked, "Then all we gotta do is take him to the bridge, untie him and—"

"Exactly!"

Doc Savage was seized and bundled out. He was borne with the greatest of speed to the ancient ship's bridge. There, they untied him. A flashlight was thrust into his hands.

"We've got you covered with guns," they told him. "Stand on the bridge and throw the light on yourself. Keep the light on, until you're sure the cops have seen you."

"And just what will refusal mean?" Doc demanded.

"It'll mean you and the rest of 'em'll get croaked!" a voice grated. "An' it'll also mean we can fight our way outta this trap!"

Doc Savage was silent for a moment, apparently considering the fate of himself and his men. Then he shrugged.

"All right," he said.

He stepped to the end of the bridge. The rusty old rail was of metal pipe, except for the top strake, which had been of wood and was still in fair shape. This presented a flat upper surface.

Doc Savage thumbed the flashlight on. He placed it on the rail. The beam was turned, not on himself, but on the men with the guns.

Then Doc vanished!

It happened in flash parts of seconds. It seemed that the light was hardly on the men before their guns roared. Yet the interval was sufficient for the bronze man, knowing exactly

what he was going to do, to move. He leaped the bridge rail-
ing over the side of the ship.

He did not, however, go completely over. Instead, he
grasped the rail, lowered himself and moved rapidly to the
left, clinging with his hands. He was in darkness, so that his
action was not observed. The manner in which he had sailed
over the rail deceived the men.

"He's in the water!" they bawled.

Chapter XX

THE BRAIN

THE men charged for the rail.

The bronze man regained the deck some distance from the
bridge. His feet touched a bit of loose wood and made some
racket, but the noise escaped notice in the confusion. Doc
picked up the fragment of wood and tossed it overside.

"There he is!" they shouted. A burst of shots followed the
splash which the chunk of wood made.

Doc moved as silently as possible. Most of the outer doors
had long since been removed from the old vessel, and he entered the first opening which he found. There was a great
deal of noise in this part of the ship. Men were rushing for
the scene of excitement.

Doc Savage descended into the lower regions of the vessel.
It was now necessary to progress by sense of touch alone, but
he made good speed.

Nearing the stateroom where the other prisoners were confined, he met two of the gang carrying flashlights. He saw
them in plenty of time, however, and lurked inside a cabin
door in wait for them.

His pounce upon them was the descent of Nemesis herself.
He managed to get an arm around the neck of each simulta-
neously. He wrenched. Their heads came together forcibly.
Each kicked once violently, then became limp.

One of the men wore a long, light topcoat and a hat. Doc
appropriated these two garments, and also one of the flash-

lights. He put that hat on his head and ran toward the prison stateroom, pulling on the topcoat.

There was a guard at the door. He was holding a flashlight on the prisoners; but when he heard Doc approaching, made a move to turn his flashlight beam in that direction.

"It's all right!" Doc said, in a voice greatly different from his normal one.

Deceived, the guard did not turn his flash on the bronze man. The fellow probably never knew exactly what happened to him. Certain it was that he did not see the metallic block of a fist which hit solidly ahead of his right ear.

The man turned a neat somersault into the room and landed flat on his back, unconscious.

An instant later, Doc Savage was untying the prisoners.

Outside, guns still banged. The men were doing some wild shooting, in hopes that a bullet would find the bronze man.

"Listen to the fireworks!" Monk squeaked, excitedly. "Boy, them cops must be cleanin' house!"

"Quite the contrary," Doc said, grimly. "There are no cops."

"Huh?"

"Their mind-reading machine picks up a man's imaginings, just as it does ordinary thought processes," Doc explained.

Monk gulped out, "You mean that business about police being posted around here was imagination?"

"It was," Doc admitted. "And it took some rather intense concentration to put it across."

Hando Lancaster heaved up, howling, "Let's get out of this! I wish I'd never invented the thing!"

"Not so loud, guy!" Monk admonished.

All of the prisoners were now untied. They crowded out into the corridor.

"We will go toward the stern," Doc said, "and try to make a get-away."

Since caution was more imperative than haste, Doc used his flashlight only sporadically. They made fair time, however. Monk and Ham brought up the rear. Jethro Mandebran and Sylvan Niles were in the middle. Hando Lancaster kept at Doc Savage's elbow, along with Johnny.

They had covered perhaps two-score yards, when Doc Savage stopped abruptly.

"Something wrong?" Hando Lancaster growled.

"Quiet!" Doc told him. "Listen!"

The others heard it then—a faint scuffling and bumping, close by.

"It's comin' outta that room there!" Monk breathed, and pointed.

Doc Savage veered toward the source of the noise. He used his flashlight. It revealed a door, or rather the opening where a door had been. He stepped through and thumbed the beam on again.

A man, thoroughly entwined with ropes, was disclosed. The fact that this man was blindfolded and gagged, made it impossible to discern his features. Doc Savage whipped forward.

The others crowded into the door, behind the bronze man, staring curiously. They had known of no other prisoners, but here was one!

Doc removed blindfold and gag from the captive, and the man's features became distinguishable.

"Young Alex Mandebran!" Monk barked.

THERE was shocked silence.

Sylvan Niles gasped, "But—but—he's their leader! How did he get here?"

Doc Savage was removing the rope from young Alex Mandebran. The man could move better under his own power.

"Alex Mandebran is *not* their leader!" Doc explained, as he worked with the rope.

Sylvan Niles gasped, "But they said that—"

"They were giving us a clever line of talk to throw the blame on Alex Mandebran," Doc Savage told her. "The real leader of the outfit was, at the time, playing the part of a prisoner with us. He was building himself an alibi in rather clever fashion."

There was a scuffle near the door.

"Grab Hando!" Doc yelled, suddenly.

"Too late!" Monk snapped. "He's running for it!"

DOC SAVAGE, rushing for the door, rapped, "We must stop him! He knows there are no police, and he will tell the gang!"

Hando Lancaster had demonstrated on other occasions that there was speed in his pipestem legs. He proved it again now. He went down the passageway with the agileness of a scared goat. Doc, putting forth his best efforts, overhauled the man, but much more slowly than was to be desired.

Hando Lancaster began to yell. The fact that his ordinary manner of speech was a howling and roaring, had given him a foghorn voice. He used it to advantage. His squalls must have carried far beyond the confines of the abandoned boat.

From on deck, forward near the bridge, shouts answered, and men could be heard charging to the assistance of Hando.

Ahead of Doc Savage, Hando Lancaster came to a sudden stop. Sensing an ominous purpose behind the move, the bronze man also halted. He dashed his flashlight beam down the corridor.

Hando Lancaster had evidently known where the jug of hydrocyanic acid had been placed. He had gotten it, was holding it in his hands.

Johnny, Monk and Ham came up behind Doc.

Hando Lancaster's men were below deck now, coming from the direction of the bows.

With fierce purpose, Hando Lancaster drew back to throw the jug of deadly acid. He was no more than fifty feet away. The jug of hydrocyanic, once he threw it, would either hit Doc Savage or burst close enough to splash the bronze man. In the cramped confines of the corridor, there would be slight chance of escaping the stuff.

Doc Savage wore low-cut shoes. They would come off without unlacing. He removed one, then the other. He placed the flashlight on the floor, so that the beam played on Hando Lancaster. With the shoes ready, he waited.

The bottle would have to be broken in mid-air with one or the other of the shoes.

Hando Lancaster seemed to be enjoying himself, and he took a long moment to get set for the throw. That was his undoing.

A gun slammed so close to Doc Savage's ear that he was almost deafened.

The jug came to pieces in Hando Lancaster's hands. Since he was holding the thing above his head at the moment, the contents deluged him, splashed over the floor.

Hando Lancaster screamed as only a man can scream when he knows he is going to die. He spun and fled. He did not, however, get far, before he went down, still shrieking— to have convulsions on the floor and eventually to die.

Doc Savage scooped up the flashlight and spun to confront Monk, who was holding a smoking revolver.

"Why didn't you wait until the thing was thrown, when no one would have been killed?" Doc Savage demanded.

"Who do you think I am, Annie Oakley?" Monk snorted. "I was lucky to hit that jug when he was holding it still in his hand."

"Where did you get the gun?"

"Off that fellow you kayoed."

"Come on!" Doc said, grimly.

They resumed their flight. Monk trailed Doc Savage a bit uneasily. Doc had an ironclad rule that no human life was to be taken by himself or his men on any occasion, whatever the provocation. Monk, the truth was, had his own idea of what should happen to gentlemen of Hando Lancaster's ilk.

A scream rasped out in the depths of the ship. It was followed by others.

Doc Savage halted again.

"They ran into the hydrocyanic vapor, not knowing it was there," the bronze man said, slowly.

Doc's party hesitated for a time, then worked toward the stern. There was nothing they could do to aid those whom the hydrocyanic was probably killing. They would probably have been shot at, anyway, had they tried to offer assistance.

Reaching the stern, they stopped. Pursuit seemed to have come to a complete end.

"How'd you come to suspect Hando Lancaster?" Monk asked Doc.

"The suicide of his business partner Castello, who headed the Castello Mining Corporation, threw suspicion on him," Doc explained. "That was about the only thing which would account for Castello's taking his own life. He had learned what Hando Lancaster was doing."

Monk sighed.

"Me," he said, "I suspected Alex Mandebran!"

Attractive Sylvan Niles came close to Doc Savage and spoke in a strained voice.

"I did not know what Hando Lancaster was really doing," she said. "I wonder if I can ever prove it?"

"I think your actions so far have proved it," the bronze man assured her.

Seemingly, Sylvan Niles did not know that Hando, using the knowledge gained from the thought machine, had made money in the stock market in the girl's name.

She was silent for a bit, and when she did speak it was in a low voice that pulsed with feeling. "Thank you."

They continued to wait, and listen. After a bit, there was a noise of a small group of men leaving the abandoned ship in a great hurry.

Monk growled, "It's my guess that we're finished with this business!"

MONK'S prediction proved to be excellent. A search of the ship disclosed that the greater number of Hando Lancaster's followers had fallen victims to the hydrocyanic vapor into which they had unwittingly plunged. The survivors had evidently fled.

Four of Hando Lancaster's strange inventions came to light, and Doc Savage set his aids to packing these for transportation. The things were too dangerous in their possibilities, to take a chance on their again falling into unscrupulous hands.

The bronze man had concluded to send them to his skyscraper headquarters for examinination. There was a possibility that they might turn out to be of some assistance to police departments. That they would never be infallible, of course, was proved by the fact that they registered *any* mental process; and imaginings were also picked up as thoughts.

The search of the old ship also brought to light other things—nearly a truckload of them. These were sealed copper boxes. They were sunk in the half-submerged bilge of the old ship, an excellent hiding place. Doc Savage retrieved and opened enough of these boxes to ascertain their contents.

Loot! Tremendous sums of it—in Liberty Bonds, securities and currency, the plunder which Hando Lancaster had taken thus far.

This stuff, of course, would have to be returned to the rightful owners.

Near dawn, after their work was finished on board the wreck, they gathered on the top deck for a rest. Because there seemed to be nothing to say, silence fell. The full loneliness of the place became impressed upon them. It was a quiet night, and the waves made no noise. Even the usual quota of insect sounds was absent.

"Blast such a place as this!" Monk complained. "I'll take mine on land or sea, not in a backwash like this!"

Monk sighed again, more loudly. Dawn was coming. It had already brought light enough for him to catch a glimpse of Sylvan Niles and young Alex Mandebran. The two young people seemed in a fair way to resume their love affair which had been broken off in England through the false accusations of Hando Lancaster.

Monk ambled over and gave Ham a jab in the ribs.

"We gotta go up in the New Jersey woods, shyster!" Monk grunted.

"Why?" Ham demanded, peevishly.

"To find my hog, Habeas, and your baboon, Chemistry," Monk explained.

"To find Chemistry," Ham corrected in his best courtroom manner. "I have no interest in your hog, Habeas!"

To the world at large, Doc Savage is a strange, mysterious figure of glistening bronze skin and golden eyes. To his fans he is the greatest adventure hero of all time, whose fantastic exploits are unequaled for hair-raising thrills, breathtaking escapes, blood-curdling excitement!

- [ ] F3969 THE TERROR IN THE NAVY (50¢)
- [ ] H5307 DUST OF DEATH (60¢)
- [ ] H5365 THE ANNIHILIST (60¢)
- [ ] F3573 THE BRAND OF THE WEREWOLF (50¢)
- [ ] H4879 FANTASTIC ISLAND (60¢)
- [ ] F3455 FEAR CAY (50¢)
- [ ] F3520 LAND OF ALWAYS NIGHT (50¢)
- [ ] H5304 LAND OF TERROR (60¢)
- [ ] F3296 MURDER MELODY (50¢)
- [ ] H5326 QUEST OF QUI (60¢)
- [ ] F3387 THE RED SKULL (50¢)
- [ ] F3441 THE SARGASSO OGRE (50¢)
- [ ] F3340 SPOOK LEGION (50¢)
- [ ] H5298 THE SECRET IN THE SKY (60¢)
- [ ] F3584 COLD DEATH (50¢)
- [ ] F3667 CZAR OF FEAR (50¢)
- [ ] F3716 FORTRESS OF SOLITUDE (50¢)
- [ ] F3782 THE GREEN EAGLE (50¢)
- [ ] F3841 THE DEVIL'S PLAYGROUND (50¢)
- [ ] H5285 DEATH IN SILVER (60¢)
- [ ] H5215 THE MYSTERY UNDER THE SEA (60¢)

8 amazing Doc Savage escapades in a boxed set!

- [ ] K5116 The Fantastic Adventures of Doc Savage ($4.80)
- [ ] NOW available from Bantam—A colorful Doc Savage poster—only $1.00 postpaid!